Ever After High™

A Wonderlandiful World

Also by Shannon Hale:

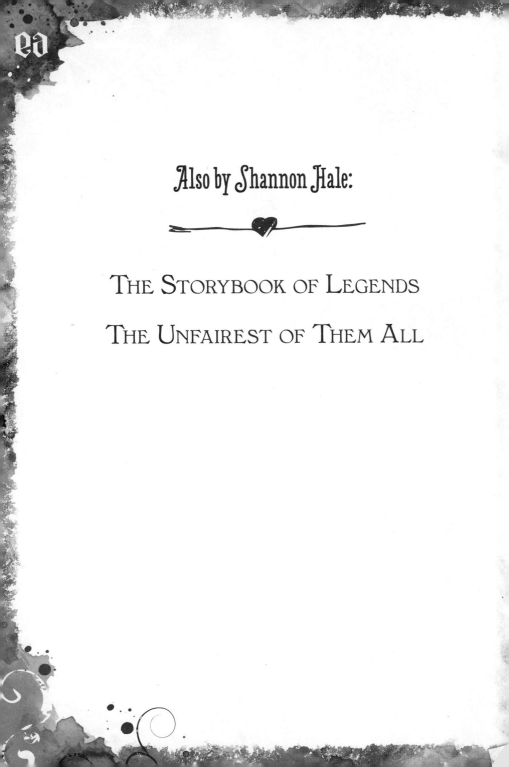

THE STORYBOOK OF LEGENDS

THE UNFAIREST OF THEM ALL

Ever After High™

A Wonderlandiful World

BY SHANNON HALE

LITTLE, BROWN AND COMPANY
New York   Boston

Copyright © 2014 by Mattel, Inc.

Excerpt from *Ever After High: Next Top Villain* copyright © 2014 by Mattel, Inc.

Little, Brown and Company

Hachette Book Group
237 Park Avenue, New York, NY 10017
Visit our website at lb-kids.com

Little, Brown and Company is a division of Hachette Book Group, Inc.
The Little, Brown name and logo are trademarks of Hachette Book Group, Inc.

The publisher is not responsible for websites (or their content)
that are not owned by the publisher.

First Edition: August 2014

Library of Congress Cataloging-in-Publication Data

Hale, Shannon.
  A wonderlandiful world / Shannon Hale.
    pages cm — (Ever after high)
  Summary: "When a mysterious being from Wonderland begins to infect
Ever After High with a strange magic, everything goes topsy-turvy. Lizzie
Hearts, Wonderland's future queen; Cedar Wood, daughter of Pinocchio; and
Madeline Hatter, heir to the Mad Hatter's Haberdashery & Tea Shoppe, seem
to be the only ones who haven't completely lost their heads. It's up to them to
save their best friends forever after from a curse that threatens to give their
school—and their lives—a very unhappy ending"—Provided by publisher.
    ISBN 978-0-316-28209-3 (hardback)—ISBN 978-0-316-28207-9
(ebook)—ISBN 978-0-316-28211-6 (library edition ebook)
  I. Title.
  PZ7.H13824Eve 2014
  [Fic]—dc23   2014014054

10 9 8 7 6 5 4 3 2 1

WOR

Printed in the United States of America

For Tessa, Ellie, and Kira
Wonder Nieces are go!

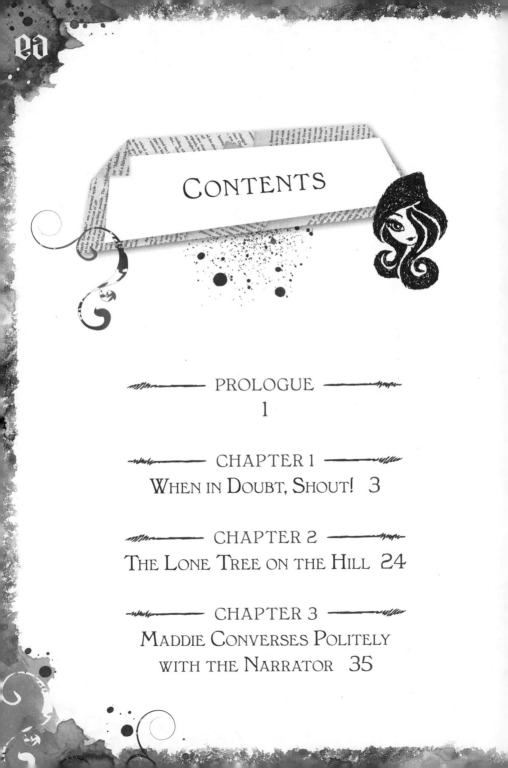

CONTENTS

Ever After High™

A Wonderlandiful World

PROLOGUE OF DOOM!

H OW MANY YEARS HAD THE GREAT JABBER-
wock spent trapped in that tiny glass Uni
Cairn prison? It had been impossible to keep track
in the shimmery, drowsy darkness, with no sun
setting, no clock ticking, no sheep counting. After
the foolish, slivy little creatures had accidentally
cracked open the Uni Cairn, the Jabberwock had
fled its prison.

It curled up in the mountains and intended to rest
for ages. Sleep. Soak power back into its fearsome
bones.

But then, the sound of breaking glass.

Not just any glass. And not another Uni Cairn. No, somewhere, an immensely powerful magic mirror shattered. The sound exploded through all of Ever After, fast and sharp like arrows. Deep in the Dark Mountains, the sound struck the sleeping beast. Nudged it. Woke it.

Awake far too early for its liking, the Jabberwock screamed its disapproval. The trees around it shook, bent, and splintered. But they shook, bent, and splintered in a completely normal way. Everything here was far too sensical. Wrong. Flat. Right-side-out. And that was infuriating.

Ever After would know its rage. It would punish the stones, the seas, and the very earth for not being as wonderlandiful as its homeland.

But first, the Jabberwock would eat. It was very, very hungry.

CHAPTER 1

WHEN IN DOUBT, SHOUT!

Lizzie Hearts, the princess of Hearts, daughter of the Queen of Hearts, heir to the throne of Wonderland's Card Castle, captain of the Ever After High Croquet Team, and hedgehog enthusiast, was holding a knife. It wasn't sharp, barely sharp enough to shout "Off with your butter!" Well, perhaps sharp enough to use on a very small man made entirely of butter. Yes, she could use this knife to behead a tiny butter man. If such a thing existed.

"Don't tell me you are packing a butter knife," Duchess Swan said as she practiced her twirls around their dorm room. Duchess, daughter of the Swan Queen, was usually dancing. Even while sleeping, she kept her toes pointed.

Lizzie stuffed the butter knife into her red-and-gold-checkered skirt pocket and felt her cheeks turn a royal flush red. In Wonderland, having a butter knife at all times just made sense—after all, one never knew when one might come upon some butter. But what made sense in Wonderland rarely made sense in Ever After. Lizzie often felt as confused as an egg full of bats.

"It's a *field trip*, for fairy's sake," Duchess was saying, doing pliés while stuffing a silver tiara and a feathery gown into her backpack. "Don't you know how to pack for a field trip?" Duchess added a pair of black satin ballet slippers. "Why, when I..."

Duchess continued to talk, but Lizzie had stopped listening. Her mother had taught her that Not Listening was a very important skill for a queen. Lizzie's hand was still in her deep skirt pocket, and she closed it around her treasured deck of playing cards. Her mother had given it to her before Lizzie escaped from Wonderland with Kitty Cheshire, Madeline Hatter, and a few others. She slid one card out of the deck and read the note scrawled by her mother's hand.

♥

Worms speak, indeed they do,
but not to such as me and you.
All they ever say is "mud mud food,"
so you need not listen good.
Practice Not Listening to worms today.
And by worms, I mean people.

♥

On each card in the deck her mother had written advice for Lizzie, designed to make her a better queen, often combined with information about how the world worked. Or how it *should* work. Even though she'd been at Ever After High for some time, Lizzie still felt incapable of understanding all the strange and infuriatingly reasonable ways of the school. Such as what one packed for a field trip.

"...a feather! Can you believe that?" Duchess was saying while brushing her long black, white, and lavender hair. Lizzie raised her hand for silence, which did not come. "And it wasn't even white, not really! It was painted, like with some kind of—"

"*Off with her head!*" Lizzie shouted.

Duchess paused, mouth open.

"Explain this field trip," Lizzie demanded.

Another of her mother's cards advised:

♥

Never ever ever ever ever ever ever ever admit
there's something you don't know.
Because you know everything.
You may have just forgotten
a piece of the everything.
Also, don't tell anyone you forgot.

♥

So Lizzie added, "Not that I don't remember ex-actly where Headmaster Grimm said we're going and why. I just want to see if you know. Naturally, it's not just a trip to a field. Um…right?"

Duchess sighed. "This is a Winds trip. Each year we visit one of the Four Winds. The West Wind was last year, remember?"

Unfortunately, Lizzie remembered that trip to the beach very well. She hadn't minded the West Wind himself, even though he kept calling everyone "dude." He hadn't looked like actual wind at all, just a man in swim trunks whose blue hair was constantly flapping in a wind no one else could feel. But the after part—the "fun" part—still gave Lizzie shudders.

The students had brought swimming gear, run in and out of the water, and thrown balls over nets as if such activities were completely normal. Meanwhile, Lizzie had sat on the sand while wrapped in her flamingo-feather-trimmed cloak, sweating. If she'd asked anyone to explain what one was supposed to do on an Ever After beach, they would know she didn't know everything—and, therefore, that she wasn't ready yet to be the Queen of Hearts. And she would disappoint her mother and fail Wonderland. So she had just sat there. Sweating. And looking as much like a queen as possible.

She fingered her feathered cloak now, unsure whether she should pack it again.

Duchess was still talking. "...his name was Zephyrus, you know? Such a nice guy for a Wind. I was thinking that Zephyrus would be such a lovely name for my destined prince. Or Ryan."

Lizzie prepped herself for more Not Listening but found she didn't quite have the energy for it.

"I think I hear a hedgehog in trouble," Lizzie said. In a queenly manner—chin up and lips stiff—she walked to the ornate, heart-shaped door on her red-and-golden side of the dorm room. The door was just her height, and, to Duchess's perpetual irritation, Lizzie was the only one who could open it. But Duchess couldn't complain. After all, the magical door had been installed by special permission from Headmaster Grimm himself.

"*Excuse* me?" Duchess said. "I was in the middle of saying something."

"You're excused," Lizzie said, and walked through the door, shutting it firmly behind her.

At first there was a chilly nothing. Lizzie's pale skin prickled with mother-goosebumps as she waited for the magic. In the time it took to inhale once, a honey-scented fog rose up, swirled, and flushed away. At her back was the door, but it wasn't attached to a wall. Lizzie was no longer in the school, transported to the edge of the school grounds and into her own personal garden.

Lizzie exhaled and felt herself relax from heavy gold crown to gold-heeled red shoes. The air in the Wonderland Grove, scented by Wonderland plants and flowers, brought to mind wet bubble gum, cold fizzy soda, and half-eaten Turkish Delight.

Lizzie strolled the crystal gravel path between well-ordered flower beds, carefully pruned bushes, and perfectly shaped trees. She let her fingers trail over leaves and flowers, greeting with a touch the flora she had planted and tended. Their magic was dimmed in Ever After—the yellow polka-dotted mushrooms that popped up between tree roots couldn't change your size, for example—but at least they all looked and smelled like home. Lizzie closed her eyes and smiled. Here, she didn't have to worry if people were watching her to see if she was acting like the proper queen her mother wanted her to be.

A squeal cut through the air. Lizzie ran to the small shack where she kept gardening tools, croquet accessories, and a few hundred spare packs of Wonderlandian playing cards. Her pet hedgehog, Shuffle, was dangling from its roof by one tiny paw. Lizzie grabbed her and stroked the prickly beast as she shivered in terror.

"Apparently I was right about there being a hedgehog in trouble," she said. "How did you get all the way up there, Shuffle-bug?"

The hedgehog said nothing, because in Ever After, hedgehogs did not talk. No hedgehogs that Lizzie had seen, anyway, and she was quite observant of all things hedgehog. In Wonderland, a hedgehog—or anything, really—might talk one day and not the next, but the talking was always possible. In Ever After, things were what they were, little changing, little speaking (Duchess being a notable exception). So she had to just imagine Shuffle expressing her thanks for the rescue, go on to gush about how much she loved Lizzie, and then give her a recipe for a delicious marshmallow-lime cobbler.

"*Roink*," said Shuffle.

"Well, yes, I suppose you do talk," said Lizzie. "Just not the way I do."

"*Roink*," whispered Shuffle.

Lizzie smiled. "*Roink*," she whispered back.

"*Tweet*," said a sparrow from the top of the shed.

A finch landed next to it.

"*Tweet*," the finch said, and the sparrow nodded at it approvingly.

A robin fluttered down to join the group. "*Tweet*," said the robin.

"I don't speak Tweet," Lizzie said.

"*TWEET*," all three birds said in unison.

"Shoo," Lizzie said, waving a hand at the tiny flock. "Go away."

The sparrow cocked its head at her.

"Look, I've got nothing against birds," Lizzie said. "It's just that in Ever After, you guys tend to bring other, larger, more demanding things with you."

In the distance, somewhere between the last Wonderlandish plant and the official school grounds, someone shouted, "Lizzie!"

"And that"—Lizzie sighed—"is exactly what I'm talking about."

Apple White, the co-president of the Royal Student Council, was running toward her in impractical red-and-gold high heels. Like Lizzie, Apple was destined to become a queen. But Apple was *nice*. It made Lizzie uncomfortable. Hadn't the Queen of Hearts warned her daughter about what is expected of a queen?

♥

A queen stands and shouts in hollow rooms when feeling faint, for she is her own echo.

She is the thing that stands between
the been and the seen,
and pushes either side wide.
A queen stands for herself,
and by herself, and on her legs.
For legs are what make her stand.
But not four legs. Or forelegs.
She also stands for land. Her land. Wonderland.
Without land, one wonders where one would stand.
Especially queens.
In summary: Push. Shout. Stand. Be a queen.

♥

"Lizzie!" Apple called again, waving now, even though Lizzie was well aware of her own name, so repeating it like that seemed unnecessary. Perhaps it was an Ever After thing. She should try it out, to make the Ever Afterlings feel more comfortable.

"Apple!" Lizzie shouted, watching Apple jog the last few yards toward her.

"Hey," Apple said, a little out of breath but with absolutely no evidence of sweat, her perfect blond curls flowing around her plump cheeks and ready smile.

"Apple!" Lizzie shouted again.

"Yeah," Apple said, clearly a little confused about something, but Lizzie felt it wasn't worth worrying about.

"Apple!" Lizzie said again, because the third time's a charm.

"Hey, I tried to find you in your room, but you weren't there, and Duchess wouldn't tell me anything." Apple held out a hand, and the finch flitted down to perch on her finger, the sparrow and robin landing lightly on her shoulders.

"She didn't tell you *anything*?" Lizzie asked. "I find that remarkable. She's always telling things, whether one wants to hear them or not."

Apple laughed. "Yes, well, but she didn't tell me anything about where you were. I guess I didn't pay attention to the rest."

Lizzie nodded. Apple must have gotten the Not Listening lesson from her mother, too. Perhaps they were more similar than Lizzie had thought.

"Anyhoo," Apple said, "I sent my sweet little bird friends to find you so that I could offer you a most hexcellent opportunity to connect with the student body, be fairy helpful, and have an incredible shared experience!"

Then again, perhaps Apple and Lizzie were just as different from each other as Lizzie had originally supposed.

"I'm busy," Lizzie said.

Apple walked past her, taking in the Grove. "This is amazing! How many different species have you planted?"

"Twenty-two," Lizzie said, her voice softening against her will, "if you count the two types of flux-berry bushes, three different Wondodendron bushes, and several subspecies of Venus Fairy Traps."

Apple crouched by a fluxberry bush, gaping as the berries changed color before her eyes. "You should totally show this place off. I think people have the wrong idea about you."

"What idea do they have?" Lizzie asked.

"Oh, I don't know, like you're often yelling, talking about chopping off heads, and altogether imperious," Apple said, petting the furry purple Wondodendron leaves.

That sounded about right to Lizzie. Loud and imperious was how books about Wonderland usually described the Queen of Hearts. Perhaps she was doing an okay job of turning into Mother after all.

So why did the thought make her feel like the last kitten left in the local village's FREE KITTENS! box?

"But you're way softer than that," Apple said, leaning over to sniff a six-headed bellflower. "I mean, you must have a soft heart and an amazing amount of patience to create and tend a garden like this! In here, it's like I'm seeing the real Lizzie."

The real Lizzie? She had clearly let her guard down for Apple to say something like that. Feeling suddenly too visible and Not Perfect Enough, she put on her queen face.

"I do not have time for whatever helpy-sharey thing you have come to enlist me in, and trying to flatter me with interest in my Grove will not change my—"

"Oooh!" Apple squealed. "Hedgehogs! You have cute little hedgehogs in here!"

"Yes," Lizzie said, grabbing one of the little creatures. She started to pet it but stopped, not wanting to appear too soft. "They make excellent weapons." Lizzie tossed the hedgehog at the garden shed. Wonderlandian hedgehogs were nearly indestructible on the quill side. That's what made them such excellent croquet balls.

"Oh! Poor little thing!" Apple gasped, running to where the hedgehog was now stuck to the shed's wall, its quills embedded in the wood. It gave Lizzie a little wave. Lizzie waved back. Clearly, Apple White didn't know *everything* after all if she thought a Wonderlandian hedgehog could get hurt from a little hurling.

"Are you okay, little guy?" Apple said, prying the beast free.

It plopped to the ground and ambled into the nearest bush.

"It looks like he is okay." Apple turned to Lizzie. "How could you? You—" Her eyebrows lifted with a thought. "Well, you are *destined* to sort of be a villain, aren't you? I can't fault you for following your destiny."

"If you haven't packed for the field trip, Apple, I think now would be a good time," Lizzie said, her discomfort growing.

"Yes! Of course! The field trip!" Apple went through the motions of dusting herself off, even though she had absolutely no dirt on her. "That's why I came! Headmaster Grimm needs you in the

Royal Student Council Room—for the, as you said, helpy-sharey thing."

"Oh!" Lizzie ran to the heart-shaped door that led back to her dorm room. "I'll meet you there."

Apple followed her. "I'll just—"

Lizzie whirled. "You'll just *nothing*!" No one but her had ever gone through the heart-shaped door.

Apple widened her eyes. She seemed almost afraid. And that was what Lizzie wanted, wasn't it? For people to be afraid of her?

Advice from one of her mother's cards:

♥

It is better to be gloved than bearded,
and better to be fearded than loved.

♥

Lizzie pulled on her black lace–hemmed gloves tighter. She affixed her most fearsome expression on her face and said to Apple, "You go on foot. I will meet you there."

She entered her dorm room and slammed the magic door behind her. Perhaps her mother would be proud. But instead of buzzing with power and joy, Lizzie felt a little lonely, as perhaps a hedgehog dangling from a garden shed might, no one near to hear its squeak.

Lizzie power-walked through the corridor, under the school's pillar trees, and down the stone steps. What could Headmaster Grimm want? She hadn't broken any rules, had she? One never knew in this un-peculiar land. After all, Maddie had nearly been banished just for trying to celebrate the Swapper-snatch Gyre. True, the Uni Cairn had tragically broken right at her feet, releasing the Jabberwock, but that hadn't been Maddie's fault. Besides, Baba Yaga said the Jabberwock would likely curl up on a mountaintop somewhere far away and sleep for years.

Just as Lizzie reached the Royal Student Council Room door, Apple flew in through a window. That is, about a hundred songbirds carried her through and set her down beside Lizzie. With wings and beaks, they arranged her hair and clothes in perfect order before flying off.

"Thank you, my feathered friends!" Apple called after them. She smiled at Lizzie as if nothing un-comfortable had passed between them and opened the door.

The headmaster was pacing on the Student Council's dais, checking his gold pocket watch. He had a firm face, steel-gray hair, and an impressive gray suit. All that grayness seemed to declare to Lizzie, *I am serious!* Beside him, Daring Charming leaned against a desk, checking his teeth in the reflection of his sword. His blond hair was combed back and gelled to within an inch of its life. Briar Beauty lay on the floor between them, dressed in hot pink and snoring sweetly. What was going on?

Timely advice from one of Lizzie's mother's cards:

♥

When in doubt, shout!

♥

"WHAT IS THIS ABOUT, HEADMASTER GRIMM?" Lizzie shouted.

Grimm winced and rubbed his ears. "Er, yes. Well, Miss Hearts, I need your help."

Aha! The shouting had worked! Her mother was a genius.

Daring swooped into a royal bow and said, "Be still, my heart! A fair princess has arrived!" And, strangely, he was looking at Lizzie, not Apple.

Daring's complimentary, showy stuff seemed to set the Ever After girls' lashes aflutter, but Lizzie raised an eyebrow.

"If your heart were still, Mr. Charming," she said, "then you would be dead."

"Excuse me?" Daring asked.

"You said 'be still, my heart,' thereby commanding your heart to stop beating," said Lizzie. "If your heart is obedient, I expect you to drop dead at my feet."

Daring stared at Lizzie. He opened his mouth and seemed surprised when a chuckle escaped it. Lizzie smirked. She didn't often hear Daring Charming chuckle.

Apple pulled some papers out from under Briar's sleeping form and handed them to Lizzie.

"'*The Tragedy of Aquilona*,'" Lizzie read. "'A play by Milton Grimm.'"

"The performance will be a delightful and surprising part of our field trip to the North Wind tomorrow," Grimm said. "However, our Aquilona has never actually practiced her part, because at every rehearsal, the actress…" Grimm nodded to Briar snoring sweetly on the floor. "We need a replacement."

A chill skipped down Lizzie's spine. Prance about in an attitude of drama before a bunch of commoners? Surely her mother would not approve. People performed for a queen, not she for them.

But she remembered a piece of her mother's playing-card advice:

♥

If you want something done right,
you must do it yourself.

♥

Of course, her mother had followed up that advice with:

♥

So make sure you personally order servants
all by yourself to do what you want done.

♥

Pfft. Not a single servant in all of Ever After waited upon her. She was constantly having to do stuff herself. Stuff like thronework. And pillow fluffing. And hedgehog hurling.

"Why me?" Lizzie asked.

"You are a Royal," Grimm said. "For this part, we need a loyal Royal. *Ahem.* Rhyme intended."

"But the field trip is tomorrow already," said Lizzie.

Apple took her hand. Instinctively, Lizzie pulled it away. She wasn't used to being touched. Apple didn't seem the least troubled.

"Lizzie, what does it say outside the Castleteria?" Apple asked. "The little yellow sign by the door that was put up last week."

"'All students are henceforth required to forgo any and all activities of war, conflict, combat, and indeed all projectile-based activities upon entering this facility,'" Lizzie quoted. "'Comestibles taking to the air by means magical or otherwise—'"

"Wow," Daring interrupted.

"You were right, Ms. White," Headmaster Grimm said.

"About what?" Lizzie asked.

"About you," Apple said. "You can memorize stuff royally fast."

Lizzie shrugged. She did have all fifty-two of her mother's cards memorized. And lots of other stuff, too, like rules and poems and recipes for weapons-grade scones. A good memory was essential for a ruler of Wonderland. In such a topsy-turvy place, someone had to remember what things were, what they were not, and what they might possibly become.

"Here." Apple took the script from Lizzie and scribbled a new first line of the play:

Aquilona: Off with her head!

"Start that way," Apple said.
Lizzie smiled, just a little.

CHAPTER 2

THE LONE TREE ON THE HILL

CEDAR WOOD STOOD ON THE LAKESHORE, wiggling her toes nervously in the sand. They made little creaking noises when they moved, like a tree bending with the wind. Cedar glanced around to see if anyone noticed. Hopper Croakington II stood next to her in frog form, tapping his webbed foot in the water, staring back at the path for his racing partner, Daring Charming, to appear. He noticed Cedar looking at him and smiled.

"Pip-pip, my little wooden foe," he said. "Good luck! It must feel daunting to compete against a Charming and a Croakington, but worry not! This is just the qualifying race. You can lose with dignity."

Cedar nodded and tried to keep her mind blank. Being cursed to speak only the truth came with a side effect: sometimes blurting out whatever was in her head at any moment.

"One question, though," Hopper said, his voice dropping in volume. "A bit personal, though. Do you mind?"

"No," Cedar said, and then, despite her best efforts, added, "I mean, I would mind if it's something awkward, because then I'd have to tell you the truth."

Hopper blinked. "Right. So—"

Kitty Cheshire flickered into visibility next to him, saying nothing.

"Er...hello, Kitty. That is, as I was saying, Cedar." His eyes twitched back to Kitty, who clearly made him nervous. Kitty just kept smiling like always.

"Yes, Hopper?" Cedar prompted.

The son of the Frog Prince rallied. "Yes, I was going to ask: Do you float? As in, being made of wood, do you have to make an effort not to sink, or does it come naturally?"

"I naturally float," she said.

"Get ready, Cedar!" a voice called from behind.

Cerise Hood was running down the cobblestone path leading to the lake, red hood covering up her white-streaked dark brown hair, red cape flapping behind her. She seemed built for athletics—tall and broad; strong, solid thighs; and intense eyes focused on her destination.

"Where the deuce is Daring?" Hopper grumbled. "He's supposed to be fast!"

Cedar's toes wiggled more frantically. She patted herself, checking to make sure she was ready for her practice swim. Her dark, wavy hair was tucked into a bunch of braids. Her swimsuit was, almost literally, a *suit*. It started high at her neck and extended all the way to her wrists and ankles. She hadn't had time to smear on her waterproofing lotion this morning, and she needed to avoid swollen joints.

"It could be that Daring found a damsel in distress in one of the trees along the path," Kitty said.

"What?" sputtered Hopper.

"It could be that I accidentally left a blond wig in

one of those trees," Kitty said, examining her nails. "It could also be that I screamed 'help' from up there, you know, before popping over here."

Cedar jogged closer to the water as Cerise ran up beside her, handing off the tightly wound waterproof relay scroll.

"I have it!" said Cedar, gripping the relay scroll. "So do I just—"

"Yes!" said Cerise. "Jump in!"

Cedar dived into the lake. She didn't even submerge, her body easily floating on the water. She supposed the water was chilly, but cold didn't bother her. Or heat. Or anything really—well, except for fire. And axes. And wood chippers. And woodpeckers, beavers, termites...

"Swim!" Cerise shouted from shore, keeping pace with Cedar on land.

Cedar swam.

"You guys are already two minutes ahead of last year's relay winners," Raven Queen called out from the opposite shore. Dressed all in purple and black with silver-studded knee-high boots, Raven didn't resemble any coach Cedar had seen before. But she'd stuck an Ever After High baseball cap onto her purple-and-black locks to look more sporty.

Cedar held up a wooden thumb and kept kicking. With Raven as their coach, Cerise and Cedar's relay team naturally became known as the "Rebel" team. Since Legacy Day, everything was becoming "Rebel" this and "Royal" that. Raven had refused to sign the Storybook of Legends and promise to become the Evil Queen like her mother, and now it seemed everyone had to take sides. Apple White, who had been devastated by Raven's refusal to sign, now led the Royals, those who wanted their fairytale destinies and pledged to someday live out their inherited stories exactly as scripted. The Rebels were following Raven's lead, vowing to write their own destinies, no matter what path their parents took.

Cedar's story wasn't as bad as some, but as the next Pinocchio, she was supposed to make lots of bad choices that would bring heartache to her kind, loving father before eventually getting turned into a real girl. To Cedar, that story never felt "just right," as Blondie Lockes would say.

"Go, Cedar, go!" a voice called from directly above her. Cedar flipped onto her back to see Cupid hovering, her pink hair billowing in the breeze made by her flapping feathered wings.

"You are amazing," Cupid said. "I'm wicked bad in the water. But you make swimming look enchantingly easy."

"It is easy," Cedar said, and then, "I wish I hadn't said that. It sounds boasty, and that's not what I mean at all." She paused. "I also wish I hadn't said that."

Cupid giggled.

"Cupid, leave her alone," shouted Cerise from the shore. "She's trying to go fast, and you're distracting her!"

"Right! Sorry! Swim enchantingly, easily on!"

Cupid flitted off, and Cedar turned back onto her stomach, paddling with all her might. Cerise was counting on her, and Cedar really hated disappointing people. It made her feel terrible, but because of her honesty "blessing" from the Blue-Haired Fairy, she was compelled to *tell* people exactly how she felt. Cedar was a fan of the truth in general, but by the godmother's wand, was it ever awkward having to volunteer the truth *all* the time! It kind of made you a weirdo.

"Shore!" and "Rock!" two people yelled at the same time, so it sounded like "Shock!" Cedar looked up midstroke and was in fact shocked as her head slammed into a large stone on the lakeshore.

Feet splashed into the water, hands helping her up and out onto the sand.

"Are you okay?" Raven asked.

"Fine, good," Cedar said. "Just embarrassed."

"There's nothing to be embarrassed about," Raven said. "You guys are still, like, a minute ahead of the best recorded time, and all you have left is the biking part."

"Where's Sparrow?" Cerise said, scanning the lakeside path.

Cedar spotted fresh bicycle tracks.

"Looks like he was here but took off," Cedar said.

"This is a disaster," said Cerise with an irritated huff and puff.

Cedar ducked her head. "Sorry." Raven had suggested that Cedar partner with Cerise and Sparrow Hood for the Glass Slipper's annual Tiara-thalon, an opportunity to get out of her art studio and make more friends. But here she was spoiling it from the start.

Raven put her hand on Cedar's shoulder. "Cerise isn't mad at you."

"What?" Cerise said, voice cracking a little. "No, no, Cedar. I'm sorry. I'm just mad at myself for thinking that I could count on Sparrow."

Dexter Charming, the younger of the Charming brothers at the school, pedaled on his royal-blue mountain bike to the group of wet, grumpy, and rebellious girls.

"Hey, what's upon-ing?" Dexter asked, skidding to a halt. "Is your practice run over? I wanted to see if I could keep pace with Sparrow."

"Looks like Sparrow got bored waiting and took off," Raven said.

"Tragic ending," Dexter said, adjusting his thick-rimmed glasses. "Do you need to borrow my bike?"

"Yeah, we do," Cedar said, unable to keep her thoughts from bursting out. "If our team's biker doesn't cross the finish line by noon, then we won't qualify to compete in the Tiara-thalon. But ... you're a Royal. I wouldn't think that a Royal would want to help Team Rebel."

Dexter shrugged. "Who cares? I mean, maybe

you care. I mean, maybe I should care…but I don't know. I feel like things are getting out of control around here, and can't a Royal still like a Rebel?…Or not *like* like, or maybe *like* like—I don't know what I'm talking about. But you can still borrow my bike for your practice and for the race itself, if you want."

Raven smiled at Dexter, and Cedar thought she saw him blush.

"Will you ride it, Raven?" Cedar asked.

"I would…" Raven examined her boots. "Should have worn my studded sneakers."

Dexter said, "I'll do it for you, Raven."

"Really?" said Cerise. "For the…er…Rebel team?"

Dexter rubbed his brown hair as if trying to smooth it flat, but it stood straight up in front. "Maybe our team will show some people that the whole Rebel and Royal thing doesn't have to be that big of a deal."

Cedar handed him the relay scroll, still wet from the lake, and he took off. Fast.

"He's good," Cedar said, watching Dexter pick up speed.

"Yes," Raven said. "Yes, he is."

"Hey, Raven," Cedar said. "Do you *like* like Dexter?"

Cerise made a muffled grunt that turned into a cough, and Raven blinked.

There was a moment of silence, and Cedar wasn't entirely sure what was going on. It could be that Raven didn't want to answer, because Cedar, being who she was, would end up telling everyone. People only shared stuff with Cedar once everyone else already knew. Even standing there under the candy-blue sky, part of a relay team, Cedar felt locked up and alone.

No one was talking, and that made Cedar lonelier than ever. Into the silence, Cedar said, "I don't want to be the lone tree on the hill."

Raven wrapped her arms around Cedar in a tight hug. "No worries, little sapling," she said. "I will always be your forest."

Cedar smiled. She noticed the creaking noise her face made whenever it carved itself into a different expression, and pulled away from Raven, not wanting her to hear it, too.

"Speaking of forests," Cedar said. "We've got a

field trip tomorrow, to the Dark Mountains, right? I'm running low on paints, and I was hoping to gather some berries there to make more. Will you guys help?"

"Totally," Cerise said.

"Sure thing," said Raven, and then her brow furrowed. "Unless Apple needs me first. She has some surprise something she's doing at the field trip that she said she might need help with if Briar falls asleep."

"That's okay," Cedar said, and it was true, but there was still a part of her that felt just the tiniest bit un-okay. There always was.

CHAPTER 3

❦

MADDIE ~~CONVERSES POLITELY~~
~~WITH~~ THE NARRATOR
Interrupts

THE MORNING OF THE FIELD TRIP DAWNED AS yellow-gold as leprechaun treasure.

Ooh, Narrator, that's a pretty image! Well, if leprechaun treasure is pretty. Is it? I haven't seen any before. Oooh! What if leprechaun treasure is actually, like, something really, really gross? That wouldn't be pretty.

Madeline Hatter, you know I can't talk to you.

Characters aren't supposed to be able to hear the Narrator, and it's so awkward for me that you can.

Mmhm, but that's called a simile, isn't it, Narrator? When you say that something is like something else to paint a picture in the reader's mind? The sun was like an egg frying on the sky, or the tea was as hot as dragon's fire, or the crab juggled like a six-legged man?

Yes, a simile, exactly. But I must get back to the narration. Many things are about to happen—

Ooh! What things? Tell, tell!

Well, the drama will really start when a frightening—wait! You're not going to get me to spoil the story, Maddie, not this time!

Aw, Narrator, you're cute as a whole bag of buttons. You're as cleverful as books that read themselves. This simile game is fun! You're as invisibilish as a ghost playing hide-and-seek. You're—

Shh. No more interruptions, please. I must return to the narration. *Ahem.*

CHAPTER 4

THE TRAGEDY OF ~~AQUILONA~~ Lizzie

THE MORNING OF THE FIELD TRIP DAWNED AS yellow-gold as leprechaun treasure. The great castle of Ever After High seemed gilded with the light. Songbirds swooped and sang, butterflies danced with fairies, goblins yawned and crept into the cellar to sleep.

In her dorm, Lizzie dressed carefully, as always, arranging her red-and-black hair under her crown. She peered at her mirror, painting a red heart around her left eye. Her mother bore a heart-shaped birthmark. Lizzie was born without the birthmark, so she drew one on each day to be a little more like her mother.

She slipped her pack of playing cards into her pocket and didn't bother to take anything else. Except for the butter knife. You could never be sure.

A field trip day was a bubbling cauldron of excitement. The corridors were raucous, the laughter constant. By the time Lizzie marched and shouted her way through the school and out to the wishing well, there was an enormous line. She could tell which students were going to visit the West Wind by their attire—all swimsuits and flip-flops, reeking of coconut sunscreen. In front of Lizzie, two fairy-godmothers-in-training prattled on endlessly about the supposedly spectacular hollowed-out mountain palace the East Wind lived in.

At last it was Lizzie's turn.

"The North Wind," Lizzie said to the fairy godmother directing traffic at the wishing well. She waved her wand, and Lizzie jumped in. After a rush of sparkly darkness and freezing-hot breezes, Lizzie hopped out of another wishing well in the Dark Mountains beyond the Dark Forest. She looked around for a royal sedan chair carried by four servants (preferably card soldiers), but when none appeared, she was forced to trudge up the mountainside like the rest of her class.

"Hey, Lizzie!" Madeline Hatter hopped up on one foot. Maddie was dressed in layers of turquoise and purple, which matched her hair colors. Her striped and polka-dotted skirts flounced with each hop. "Hop with me!"

Maddie held out her hand. Lizzie's hand twitched, almost reaching back. But readily her mind called up her mother's advice:

♥

A ship is only as floaty as its leakiest timber,
and friends are the leakiest timber of all.
Sail not on the Friend Ship, Lizzie,
lest you drown in an ocean of tears!

♥

"A princess of Wonderland never hops," said Lizzie.

She walked through the forests of the mountain path alone.

No blue-skinned North Wind (in swimming trunks or otherwise) waited at the top of the mountain. Instead an amphitheater of log benches faced a small stage.

"Ooh, are we watching a play?" said Maddie. "Tea-riffic!"

"This is just right," said Blondie Lockes, settling onto a bench alongside other Royals, including Briar Beauty and Holly O'Hair.

Lizzie started for the backstage. Behind the curtain, Apple and Daring were slipping on costumes over their clothes.

"Break an egg," Lizzie said to Apple.

"Excuse me?" Humphrey Dumpty squeaked as he passed by, his white-pale cheeks turning so pink he seemed to be dyed.

"It's *leg*," Apple whispered. "Break a *leg*."

"Oh," said Lizzie. "That's actually much better."

"Now, students, quiet down, please," Headmaster Grimm was saying on the other side of the curtain. "You're probably wondering, 'Where is the North Wind, and what is this beautiful forest amphitheater?' And perhaps even, 'I bet Headmaster Grimm is skilled in the theater arts, and when will we see an example of his genius?'"

Someone in the audience shouted something Lizzie couldn't make out.

"No, Mr. Hood, you will not be able to meet and speak with the North Wind, as you did last year with the West Wind—or the *beach dude*, as you call him. The Winds *are* part of the magnificent heritage and history in Ever After. But the reason why you can't speak with the North Wind herself is a tragedy, one I fear you *all* need to hear, especially now."

Lizzie straightened her crown. It wasn't her tall gold one with ruby red hearts that just screamed "Wonderland" (sometimes literally). This was the costume crown of Princess Aquilona, and while a shoddy representation of true royalty, it was still a crown and should be respectably oriented.

"To best communicate why the North Wind, though present, can no longer speak with humans, I have written a play," said the headmaster. "Behold, *The Tragedy of Aquilona*, performed by the Ever After High Royal Players!"

The curtain rose to thunderous applause. Faybelle Thorn shouted "Boo!" so loudly and brightly it sounded like a cheer. Lizzie, flustered, yelled the first line of the play that Apple had written for her, and the crowd silenced.

Grimm lifted his arm up grandly and intoned, "Long ago, Boreas, the great North Wind, ruled the mountaintops."

The headmaster's voice was suddenly high-pitched and trembly, like someone trying to sing soprano who really shouldn't.

"Why is he talking like that?" Lizzie heard Maddie whisper loudly from the audience. "Is someone choking him?"

Daring marched forward with his typical easy-going yet kingly demeanor. He was dressed in a white billowy wind costume that didn't completely cover his muscles. Some of the girls in the audience squealed.

"I, Boreas, rule the winds of the North!" Daring announced.

"The nature of wind is to be wild," Grimm said.

Apple rushed onstage in a fringed blue cloak. The audience applauded, several shouting, "Apple White! It's Apple White!"

"I am the wild wind," Apple howled. A few

birds in the surrounding forest sang out in happy response.

"Shh, she's not talking to you," Maddie whispered at the birds.

"But Boreas was the shepherd of all the winds of the North, directing them hither and yon," Grimm continued in a tight, squeaky voice.

"I shepherd you," Daring said, pointing at Apple. "Go hither! And yon!"

Someone in the audience actually did yawn at this point. Lizzie had to admit the lines Grimm had written were a little flat.

"Boreas's companion in his great work was his daughter, Princess Aquilona," Grimm said.

"I am Princess Aquilona," Lizzie said, her fists on her hips.

The line was longer, but Lizzie deemed it too boring to finish. The headmaster waited for the rest, but Lizzie just folded her arms.

Grimm cleared his throat. "Princess Aquilona was destined to take on her father's responsibilities, but she refused."

"I will not take on your responsibilities," Lizzie said, pointing at Daring.

Daring opened his mouth in a parody of shock. "Ridiculous! It is your destiny! To deny your destiny would destroy everything!"

"Then I shall leave forever and go where the North winds cannot travel!"

The audience gasped. Lizzie smiled. Maybe this strutting-about-a-stage business wasn't so bad. She glanced at the anxious face of Headmaster Grimm for inspiration and decided to make up a few more lines. "I will not be the daughter who does nothing but watch her wrinkled father writhe with the agony of age and death, your voice slowly becoming more nasal and oddly high-pitched, as if you were being strangled by a possum or a really weak octopus or something."

Daring pressed his lips together, valiantly attempting to hold back a laugh, and ultimately failing.

He covered his face with his hands, and Lizzie knew she must do something to save the play.

"Do not blubber so, Father. When you stop weeping, I will be gone," Lizzie said.

Headmaster Grimm cleared his throat and lowered his voice to its natural pitch.

"And so, Aquilona ran away to be selfish,

ignoring her great destiny so she could do whatever selfish things she wanted. Selfishly." Headmaster Grimm looked significantly at Raven Queen, who was sitting in the back row of the amphitheater. Raven rolled her eyes.

"Meanwhile," Grimm continued, "Boreas got old."

Daring pulled a white beard from his pocket, stuck it to his face, and began to shuffle around.

"And died," said the headmaster.

"I die!" Daring collapsed to the floor in a heap.

"Without a shepherd, the winds tore up trees and hassled hills."

Apple, her wind cloak flapping, danced around, spinning and leaping across the stage, shouting "*Whoosh*" and "*Boom*" and "*Rustle rustle rustle.*"

"The winds, wanting a shepherd, blew all the way to Aquilona. But Aquilona was too selfish to claim her destiny, as previously mentioned."

Apple and Lizzie spun in the circles they had practiced, but Lizzie was not as good at remembering steps as words, and the choreographed dance turned into a sprawling slap-fight. From the floor, "dead" Boreas started to chuckle.

Lizzie shrugged into a ragged blue cloak like Apple's.

"In her struggle against the wind, Aquilona was stripped of her body, becoming wind herself," said Grimm. "She had no body after that, and without a mouth, you can't talk. And that is sad. And it was her own fault. So be warned: Those who run from their own destiny just might be chased down and turned into wind." He cleared his throat again and added grandly, "Or something! The end."

The headmaster began to applaud, and about half the audience followed his lead. The other half just silently glared, so Lizzie glared back until the curtain fell.

Daring laughed, his fake beard wiggling. "'A really weak octopus?' I just about lost it out there!"

"You did lose it," Lizzie said.

"Great job improvising, Lizzie," Apple said. "Turning his laughter into tears was perfect."

"Yes, turning laughter into tears is a skill I learned from my mother."

"I think your mother would have loved your performance," Apple said, patting Lizzie on the shoulder and heading off the stage. Lizzie held her breath, surprised by a knot of emotion in her throat.

Daring followed Apple. Lizzie heard him mutter "strangled by a possum" under his breath, letting out another chuckle.

Lizzie stayed in the quiet behind the curtain, fingering her ragged blue cloak. She was a princess separated from her kingdom, just like Aquilona. All portals between Ever After and Wonderland had been magically sealed ever since Raven's mother, the Evil Queen, went royally off script and infected it with some magical contagion. If the greedy witch hadn't rebelled and tried to take over everyone else's story, Lizzie would be home right now.

Unlike Aquilona, Lizzie yearned for her destiny. But cut off as she was, how could she become like her magnificent mother? If only she could be so scary and large and...and loud! If only she could live with Mother at home, where everything made its own kind of wonderlandiful sense, and rabbits talked and people didn't unless they were offering you cake and tea, Your Highness.

What if she was trapped in Ever After forever after? One day her mother would need Lizzie to take over, and if she couldn't get back...would a pack of wild playing cards worm their way into Ever After and steal away her body, just like the winds did to Aquilona? Would they carry Lizzie back, bodiless and mouthless, as insubstantial as a wind? The thought was terrifying.

She wished she had brought her hedgehog, Shuffle, with her. Even if it was unqueenly, just then Lizzie really needed a cuddle.

CHAPTER 5

A BABY BANDERSNATCH

WHEN THE CURTAIN LOWERED, CEDAR WAS holding her wooden hands before her, though she couldn't bring herself to clap.

"Um, that was a bit obvious, and I can't lie," Cedar said.

"Yep," said Raven Queen, her shoulders slumped.

Cedar dropped her hands. "Headmaster Grimm might as well have called the play *This Story Is a Warning to All Rebels about the Evil Consequences of Not Fulfilling Your Destiny—I'm Looking at You, Raven Queen.*"

Raven nodded. But she un-slumped her shoulders. "I'm not going to let him get me down anymore. I *am* okay with myself and my destiny-less future, and I'm ninety percent sure that I won't be turned into wind if I don't turn evil and try to poison Apple. Even so, I could really use a laugh about now. I'm going to go find Maddie. Be right back."

Raven sprang away.

On the bench in front of Cedar, Blondie Lockes whispered something to Briar Beauty. Briar snorted, bending at the waist and wiping laugh tears from under her pink crownglasses. Blondie giggled, hiccuping. Just hearing her friends laugh brought a creaky smile to Cedar's face.

"Hey, what are you guys laughing about?" Cedar asked, plopping down beside them, her legs clicking against the hard bench.

"Well, Blondie was just telling me—" Briar began, but Blondie elbowed her. "*Oof!* Blondie, what are you . . ."

Blondie nodded in Cedar's direction, opening her eyes wide in warning.

"Oh, right," said Briar. "Um, nothing, Cedar.

Never mind. I just…sorry, girl, I'd better not repeat it to you. You understand."

"Sure, I understand." Whatever it was, it was a secret. "Although I get why no one wants to share secrets with me, when you do that, I still feel whittled to my heartwood. Sorry! I couldn't help saying that. And also, Blondie, there's a huge black cricket stuck in your curls. Sorry, couldn't help that, either! Never mind. I'm going."

Cedar ran off, Blondie's horrified shrieks fading behind her.

A few minutes later, Raven found Cedar knee-deep in the scratchiest, meanest, most villainous blackberry bramble Cedar had ever found.

"What's up, Cedar?" Raven asked.

Cedar wiped her dry wooden cheeks. She felt like she was crying. A knot of sadness tightened in her chest where her heart would be, running up into her head with a burning, uncomfortable heat. But no tears fell from her carved eyes. It was just her magic-enhanced imagination.

"Oh, you know," Cedar said, shrugging as if it were unimportant. "Puppet girl is cursed to blab, so *real* girls can't confide in puppet girl, yadda yadda yadda."

"I'm sorry, Cedar," said Raven. "But...hey, why are you in the middle of a blackberry bush?"

Cedar held up a handful of dark purple berries. "For paints, remember? I like to make my own. The colors are rich and natural and uneven and unexpected and just luscious! I found some black walnuts—their shells make beautiful black paint— and I even found some turmeric for yellow."

She reached into the thicket for a fat berry, so ripe it was black. Thorns big as shark teeth scratched at her brown arms, but Cedar didn't feel a thing. She didn't even feel a thing as something lurking inside the bramble took offense at her probing arm and attacked. When she lifted her hand up again, the something was stuck to her. Furry and fat, like a dog-sized guinea pig, the thing's two rows of teeth-big-as-thorns were now clamped to her forearm.

"Oh," said Cedar.

"Whoa!" Raven stumbled back with her hands out, as if ready to cast a spell. "What *is* that?"

Cedar shook her arm, but the beastie didn't

budge. A pale green gas leaked from its nether end, and the girls turned their heads and gagged.

"That…smells…like a *very* bad ending!" said Raven.

Cedar nodded. She *could* smell things (unfortunately, at the moment)—or at least, the magic that made her alive enhanced her ability to *imagine* smells, just as it allowed her to imagine joy and sadness, fear and excitement. But the magical imagination didn't allow her to experience sickness or pain—not even from the bite of the toothy creature clamped to her wooden arm. Still, that didn't mean she wanted to keep it there.

She fought her way out of the blackberry bramble, and they ran back toward the amphitheater.

"Headmaster Grimm! Madam Baba Yaga! Help!" Raven called out.

"Um…something appears to be biting my arm," Cedar said softly. "I didn't want to make a fuss, but…"

"What is that creature?" the headmaster said, his normally robust voice a mere whisper.

Baba Yaga floated forward, sitting cross-legged on her levitating stool. Her fierce eyes and determined nose and chin made her seem formidable. She pushed her tangled gray hair out of her face and squinted. "It looks like a bandersnatch, but that's impossible. There are no bandersnatches in Ever After."

Baba Yaga took a deep sniff of the pale green gas and then smacked her lips as if trying to identify a peculiar taste. Cedar winced. She heard Raven behind her trying not to gag too loudly.

"It *smells* like a bandersnatch," said Baba Yaga. "Or perhaps a thing wearing bandersnatch perfume."

"Yeah, that's sure to be the hot new scent this spring," said Briar, her nose plugged. "Bandersnatch perfume—for those special occasions when you want everyone to run away screaming."

"Um…could you maybe pry it off my arm?" Cedar asked.

"Hold your piglets, Ms. Wood. I'm still investigating," said the old sorceress.

Cedar nodded. And considered maybe lying down and dying on the spot. All her classmates were staring at her. And she had a smelly, sticky beastie clamped on her arm. Cedar imagined the warm prickle of a blush in her cheeks, but she knew her cheeks remained the same shade of warm brown.

"Doesn't that hurt?" she heard someone whisper.

"Those teeth are, like, an inch long," someone else whispered.

"Yeah, but she's, you know, made of wood."

"I never realized she was *that* weird."

"No kidding."

Cedar closed her eyes. Maybe if she tried really hard, she could grow into a tree and disappear behind a wall of leaves. Or maybe if she tried even harder, she could wish herself real like everyone else.

Please, please, please, Blue-Haired Fairy, please make me real now. Please don't make me wait any longer or follow a choiceless destiny to get my Happily Ever After. I just want to be normal. Please …

"Aha!" Baba Yaga shouted, startling Cedar's eyes open. The old sorceress mumbled a spell, then shot mustard-yellow light from her hands, and the bandersnatch began to vibrate. With a noise like a soufflé popping in the oven, the bandersnatch transformed.

"Oh!" said Ashlynn Ella. "A fuzzy, cuddly bear cub! Look at you, sweetie pie!"

She pranced forward and began to pet the cub. Which was still clamped to Cedar's arm.

"The question is," said Baba Yaga, "why was a bear cub transformed into a baby bandersnatch?"

"It's so cute!" said Ashlynn. "What are you saying, cutie sweetie-bear? I can't hear you when you've got an arm in your mouth."

"Uh…" said Cedar.

"But…isn't a bear cub, I don't know, dangerous or something?" Raven asked.

"Not nearly so dangerous as your basic fire-breathing dragon," said Daring, "of which I've battled dozens."

Several girls sighed dreamily.

"Who's scared of a teddy bear?" said Faybelle Thorn.

"I am and not embarrassed to admit it," said Hunter Huntsman, putting his fists on his hips. His hair—styled in a sort of relaxed Mohawk—rippled in the breeze. "A bear cub is extremely dangerous not for itself but for who is nearby."

"Like it's mother?" Apple squeaked, staring at something in the distance.

"Exactly, Apple, like the cub's mother," said Hunter. "Um…Ash, you should probably leave it alone. If its mother is nearby, she might misunderstand and fear we're harming her cub."

"Nonsense," said Ashlynn, scratching behind the cub's ears. "I'd just explain to her the situation."

"In my experience," Daring said, sharpening his sword on a rock, "a mother bear mauls first and listens to lengthy explanations second."

"Uh…" said Cedar again. Baby bear/bandersnatch drool had covered her arm and was dripping into a puddle at her feet.

"Hey, bear," whispered Blondie, crouching down and whispering in its ear. "Where's the porridge? You and your folks have an unsupervised porridge-filled cabin stashed nearby? Come on, talk."

"Why a baby bandersnatch?" Baba Yaga was asking herself, tapping the wart on her chin with her finger.

"We should let the little fella go," Hunter said. "The momma bear could be mighty angry."

"Or she could, oh, I don't know, also be transformed into a bandersnatch?" suggested Apple.

Apple pointed. Cedar looked.

A momma-bear-sized bandersnatch was lumbering

toward them, drool oozing out of her spiky-toothed jaw, trails of curling green gas sputtering from her nether end, generally resembling a giant people-eating guinea pig that was having a really bad day.

She stood on her hind legs and grunt-roared.

"Off with its head!" shouted Lizzie.

Daring drew his sword with a flash of steel and an equally brilliant flash of a white-toothed smile.

"I'm just the prince for the job," he said.

Lizzie smiled in surprise that someone was actually taking her seriously. Daring winked.

Students screamed and ran, but Cedar still had a bear cub latched to her arm. She yanked at it. "Come on, teddy-weddy, just let go of me, please."

"Fear not," said Daring. "I'll protect you!"

"As will I!" Hunter loosed the ax from his belt and struck the Huntsman-To-the-Rescue Pose, fists on hips, shoulders thrown back, feet apart. From nowhere, trumpets blasted a heroic fanfare. Hunter nodded to the magical trumpet tune. He had, no doubt, heard it many times in his life.

"Headmaster, I don't like this," said Baba Yaga, sniffing the air.

"Don't be alarmed, fair—uh, noble sorceress," said Hunter. "We are well-schooled in defending damsels—uh, anyone—from ferocious beasts."

The trees around the momma bandersnatch shook. Yellow eyes lit up the shadows, and a herd of bandersnatches lumbered out. Cedar counted…nine, ten, eleven…*fourteen* full-size bandersnatches, eyes glowing, mouths drooling, nethers gassing.

"Yes, that's what I don't like," Baba Yaga muttered.

Students began to scream.

"Magic is afoot!" cried Professor Jack B. Nimble.

Baba Yaga cast a magical barrier, encaging the bevy of bandersnatches inside a sparking yellow dome. The bandersnatches grunt-roared and clawed at the magical cage, sparks flying from their paws. Cedar wondered if the cage would hold.

"Students, get out of here!" Headmaster Grimm shouted.

"Help?" Cedar whispered.

"Let! Go!" said Raven. She zapped the bear cub with a bolt of purple magic, and the cub squeaked and opened its jaws. Cedar set it down, and it galloped back toward the momma bandersnatch.

And still the bandersnatches advanced, the magical dome sparking and twinkling, its yellow color fading.

"Go straight to Ever After High and do not leave that building until we return!" the headmaster shouted.

Mr. Badwolf dropped to all fours and transformed into his wolf shape, growling, his black lips trembling. He turned to howl something over his shoulder.

"Okay!" Cerise Hood answered back. She grabbed Raven's and Cedar's hands. "We need to get out of here. Now."

Cedar had never run so fast, partly because she was fleeing a mountaintop crawling with strange, growling, sticky, pungent monsters, but mostly because Cerise Hood was dragging her along at her own speed. And by the Blue-Haired Fairy's wand, that girl could run.

Madeline Hatter was skipping beside them.

"How are you skipping so fast?" Cedar asked, her words shaking with the force of her pounding feet.

"I don't know," Maddie said, bounding along, not at all out of breath. "I'd never tried speed-skipping before, but I thought this was the perfect time for it. I am now making a point to not ask you if speed-skipping is impossible in Ever After, because if it is, Cedar will have to tell me the truth and then it might stop working. So, what's going on, anyway?"

"We're not really sure," said Raven.

"Oh, good," said Maddie. "It's a relief when everyone else is as confuse-boggled as I am. I feel so cozy, like a bundle of puppies in a box."

"That's cozy?" Cerise huffed.

Maddie giggled. "It is if you're one of the puppies. And if you're confuse-boggled, of course. If you *know* you're in a box, then you start thinking things like 'why am I in a box?' and 'who put me here?' It just makes you nervous. I, for one, am glad we don't know we're in a box."

"*Oh,*" Cedar said in a small voice. She didn't feel cozy at all.

CHAPTER 6

MADDIE ~~TRIES~~ *Fails*

TO JUST LISTEN QUIETLY

THE JOURNEY DOWN THE MOUNTAINSIDE was fraught with peril, mostly in the form of Briar Beauty. Apple White naturally took the lead, searching for sensible paths through thickets and down ledges. But Briar, her best friend forever after, was constantly picking more "interesting" paths.

"Come on, this way looks fun!" she said, grabbing Apple's hand and nearly vaulting with her over a cliff.

"Briar," said Apple, "perhaps a good goal would be not only to make it down the mountain, but also make it down alive."

"Don't be such a snooze." Briar lifted her crownglasses to look her friend in the eye. "We're fleeing a bloat of bandersnatches, hurtling ourselves over unfamiliar terrain in a gasping fight for our very lives. This is, like, the best chapter ever after."

Briar grabbed a clutch vine and swung over a boulder.

Blondie Lockes held up her MirrorPad, filming Briar's daring moves and the dark shadows of the forest, and narrating in an ominous voice. This adventure was going to make a hexcellent episode of her MirrorCast show.

Madeline Hatter, as the only character who could hear the Narrator, was listening intently to the narration. But she did *not* interrupt. Because she had promised so faithfully she would not interrupt anymore.

That's right, cutie-patootie Narrator. You'll get no interrupting from me!

Ashlynn and Hunter kept "accidentally" brushing against each other as they walked, the backs of their fingers knocking together, their knuckles grasping, until Duchess Swan finally yelled, "Oh, just hold hands, already! Everyone knows you're dating!"

Humphrey Dumpty mumbled rhymes to himself as he walked—or wobbled, actually, his thin legs trembling dangerously with each step. For the field trip, he'd completely encased himself in a thick coat of Bubble Wrap. Just in case.

Raven Queen and Dexter Charming chatted as they jogged through the woods, playing a game called What's More Evil?

"A pinecone is more evil than a pine needle," Raven said.

"Really?" Dexter said. "What about pine needle versus pine sap?"

"Um, pine sap," said Raven. "So what's more evil, pine sap or squirrel?"

"Squirrel, definitely," said Dexter.

Kitty Cheshire was—

"Wishing to remain private, thank you," said Kitty.

Oh! I didn't realize Kitty could hear me, too!

"Me neither!" said Maddie. "That's breakfast-tastic, Kitty!"

Kitty hissed.

Very well. *Ahem.* Lizzie Hearts kept to the front of the group, keeping pace with Apple, correcting all her decisions, and declaring things like "This way!" and "That way!" and "By the way!"

"Relax, Lizzie," said Briar. "Apple is in charge, and she's leading us just fine."

"One does not order a crown princess of Wonderland to relax!" said Lizzie.

"This isn't Wonderland, so stop trying to rule."

Lizzie stiffened everywhere—her shoulders, her spine, and especially her upper lip—and wished very hard she had an army of card soldiers at her command.

Madeline Hatter had begun playing leapfrog with Hopper Croakington II. Or so she thought. Hopper wasn't actually playing.

He's not? Oh, thank you, Narrator. That's why

he keeps glaring with the beady eyes and pouty lip and grumbles of "Why do you keep vaulting over my head?"

Maddie! You were doing so well at not interrupting.

Why, thank you, Narrator, dear, and that is why I'm barely interrupting at all. I learn so much about narration by listening to you, you know, such as how you're using this travel time to give us updates on all the main characters, revealing more about them through descriptions of what they're doing. How cleverful!

Thank you. It's a basic technique I learned in Narration School. But I really shouldn't—

I know, I know, no more with the barging and the pestering and the mouth flippy-flapping. Narrate on! Ooh, wait, one quickish question first.

Maddie, you know I can't answer your questions.

Well, it's just that a baby bear was bandersnatched, and either the big bears were bandersnatched, too, or there were actual true bandersnatches back there. And a bandersnatch is a Wonderlandian beast! So what are they doing in Ever After?

Um…

You know, don't you?

Er…

Come on, just a hint. You're so good at accidentally giving me teensy-weensy-bleensy hints.

Not this time! This Narrator refuses to be tricked! This Narrator is a shining example of rule-following technique! So, let's fast forward…. The group finally reached bottom, made their way to the nearest wishing well, and wishing-welled it back to Ever After High. Okay, then, next chapter!

CHAPTER 7

A TWISTED KIND OF WONDER RUN!

THE GREAT JABBERWOCK, TERROR OF WONDER-
land, was still grumpy. It had been having such
a frabjous dream of buttered bandersnatches when
that crashing, smashing, bitter-bashing sound of a
broken magic mirror had torn it away. Now it was
awake and trapped in Ever After, a land entirely
without bandersnatches, buttered or otherwise.

The bears had tasted too sweet, not nearly crunchy
enough, and more like meat than madness. After the
Jabberwock's magic melted away their bear-ness
and filled in the holes with bandersnatch-ness, the

taste had improved, though they still got stuck in the Jabberwock's gullet.

Too long it had been caged, trapped, and cut off from Wonderland. Its magic needed recharging.

The Jabberwock leaped from treetop to treetop. It could fly, but flight was exhausting in the thin air of this not-home place, and it was still tired. It yawned angrily, breath stinking of decaying magic and the meat of false bandersnatches.

The beast had gotten lost from Wonderland long ago, but its bowels were still pulsing with wonder, though a rotting, twisted kind of wonder. Its hot breath slurped and crawled out of its mouth, transforming whatever it touched. The Jabberwock exhaled, and the tree bending beneath its weight brightened to a vivid green and sprouted pumpkins instead of pinecones. The tree was not exactly what it would have been in Wonderland, but at least it was closer. Could the beast alter this un-peculiar land entirely? Make it more like home? No, not without more power.

The Jabberwock caught a whiff of tiny Alice-things fleeing the far edge of the forest. It smiled, its gray lips curling around a huge set of buckteeth.

The Card, the Cat, and the Hatter were nearby. It could smell them. It could feel the fresh Wonder emanating from their bodies. Wonder it would need if it was to shape this world to its liking.

The Jabberwock heaved up and took flight. Its massive, batlike wings shook the air, its deep purple shadow sending the forest creatures shivering into holes. It dived, mouth open, claws out ready to seize, when suddenly the Card, the Cat, and the Hatter disappeared into a wishing well. Vanished. Too fast, as if the story they were in had suddenly sped up, pages flipping faster than the narration should allow.

The Jabberwock reeled in the air, skronking with rage. It would stalk these Wonderlings. It would follow them wherever they went, and one by one it would squeeze every last drop of Wonder from their bones.

And then, maybe, it would eat them.

CHAPTER 8

WONDER ~~WORMS~~ People ARE GO!

"ORMS!" LIZZIE YELLED THE MOMENT SHE emerged from the wishing well on the grounds of Ever After High.

"What?" said Cedar.

"Where?" said Apple with a small shudder.

"Gross!" yelled Blondie.

"Yay!" said Maddie.

"Um," said Raven, "what worms, Lizzie?"

"And by worms, I mean people!" Lizzie shouted, hoping the strength of her mother's words would clarify things. She noticed that the confused stares only got confused-er.

"And by people," Lizzie continued, "I mean *Wonder* people. Er...I mean Kitty and Maddie. The Wonderlandians."

"Wonder Worms are go!" shouted Maddie, striking an action pose and then wiggling toward Lizzie. "Lady Catworm!" Maddie called to Kitty Cheshire, who hadn't moved an inch. "Make haste! We have been summoned!"

Kitty shrugged and disappeared, reappearing beside Lizzie.

"Hatworm and Catworm at your service, O Lizard Queen," Maddie said, giving Lizzie a wiggly bow.

"Don't call me that," Lizzie and Kitty said in unison.

Maddie straightened from the wormy stance. "Fine, party poops. What's the story?"

"I have something to discuss with both of you," Lizzie said, turning her back on them. "Let's go to the Grove."

"To the Grove, Catworm!" Maddie shouted heroically, and was rewarded with a hiss just as Kitty popped out of sight.

Lizzie breathed in as they left the school grounds and crossed into the Grove. Some days the rich, candied scents made her heart feel light and floaty as bubble birds. Sometimes the smells made her feel achy for home, as heavy and slow as a steel scarecrow. Today she felt nervous and jittery as if she had swallowed handfuls of live hornets.

Which she hadn't, just to clarify. One never knew with Lizzie.

"Citizens of Wonderland," Lizzie began.

Kitty looked over her shoulder, as if expecting more people to be there.

"As the representatives of our world in exile, it is our responsibility..." Lizzie was already bored with her own speech. She sighed. "Look, there were bandersnatches up there. I am certain that when we escaped Wonderland with the White Queen and Maddie's dad, no bandersnatches sneaked out with us." Were the ways to Wonderland reopening? Or had the bandersnatches found a secret way out and come looking for the lost Wonderlandian princess? Hope shivered in Lizzie.

Kitty purred, "I know of something else Wonderlandian here without permission."

"She means the Jabberwock," Maddie whispered.

"No, I don't!" Kitty's pale purple hair seemed fluffier, standing on end at the mention of the monster. She hissed, "Don't say its name out loud! I just meant the jubjub bird I was chasing on the mountaintop during that riddle-diculous play."

"A jubjub bird, too? Maybe we should talk to the White Queen," Maddie said.

"Very well," Lizzie said. "I'm glad I was able to get you to that conclusion. We will find the White Queen and demand of her an explanation."

"Or we could just ask," Maddie said.

"Or we could just ask!" Lizzie shouted as if it were a battle cry, pointing her scepter at the school.

They headed to the White Queen's office. Empty. They investigated the faculty lunchroom. Void. They peeked into likely classrooms. Nil. Then they began to get creative.

Sometime later, Maddie flung open the last stall door in the teachers' restroom. *"Aha!"* she shouted, but no one was there.

"She's hiding from us," Lizzie said. "The White Queen must know something and knows that we know she knows and wants to keep the knowing from us."

"But how can she if we already know she knows?" Maddie asked.

"The *extra* knowing," Lizzie said, nodding wisely. "The knowing about why there are bandersnatches and jubjub birds. Not the knowing that she knows."

"Oh," said Maddie. "So she's hiding from us. Good hiding."

"Too good!" Lizzie shouted. "I won't allow it! People can't just disappear!"

At that, Kitty disappeared.

"Present company excepted, of course," Lizzie muttered.

Kitty reappeared sitting on the bathroom counter. "Searching for the White Queen has been fun and all, especially the bit where Lizzie got stuck in the crawl space, but you'll never find her. You've probably noticed there are lots of people not at the school today."

"I assumed they were hiding like the White Queen," Maddie said, "to make this game of hide-and-seek more fun."

"She wasn't playing hide-and-seek," said Kitty.

Maddie threw up her hands. "Am I expected to keep track of every game and who is and isn't playing all the time?"

"The faculty and most of the students are still on their field trips," Kitty said, pulling out her Mirror-Phone to check her teeth. "Only our group came back early."

"I know that, of course. I just wanted to make sure you knew it, too." Lizzie's eyes narrowed. "But you didn't see fit to tell us this before because...?"

"Because watching you two run about like madwomen is fun."

"She does have a point," Maddie said.

Lizzie dialed the White Queen on her Mirror-Phone. No answer. Her voice mail picked up.

"*I am busy right now*," said the White Queen's recorded voice. "*Please call back ten minutes ago.*"

The door to the restroom pushed open.

"Here you are!" said Briar. "Everyone's meeting in Apple and Raven's dorm room. Some of the students are hextremely upset about what happened on the mountain, and Apple thought some soothing talk could help."

"Okay!" Maddie said, un-straightening her hat and hopping out the door.

"Soothing talk?" Kitty asked. "Royals and Rebels together, sharing nonjudgmental and openhearted opinions?"

"Totally," Briar said.

"I'm there," Kitty said, fading until all but her mouth remained. "There's bound to be a tasty fight," the smiling mouth said, and then it, too, disappeared.

"I don't see how sitting around babbling could be soothing, let alone productive," Lizzie said.

"Come on, Lizzie," said Briar. "I'll be there, so it's sure to be a blast!"

Briar was always throwing parties where Lizzie would stand awkwardly in the corner, shouting things like "Fetch me a flamingo!" or "Stand back, peasant!" in reply to any small talk. Mother would declare all those bumbling partygoers beneath the Princess of Hearts and not worth her time, and yet Lizzie spent those parties secretly, silently, carefully wishing that she were one of the girls on the dance floor, laughing with Briar. Lizzie opened her mouth to tell Briar that but found herself shouting, "Off with your head!"

"Okay, then. See you fairy soon," Briar said, throwing down a skateboard and skating down the corridor.

Lizzie drew a card from her mother's deck. Her mother's words would give her strength, courage, and direction.

♥

Already Been Chewed food (hereafter referred to as ABC food) can appear appetizing, but not for such as you. Eat no ABC food today.

♥

Hmph. That didn't seem particularly applicable. Lizzie flipped through a few more.

♥

Frogs are mostly faces.
Notice a frog today and make a face.

♥

ON WITH ITS HEAD!
JK. ☺ Behead something today!

♥

Rugs are the unnatural spawn of Rabbits and Hugs. Beware rugs. (Could also be Rubber and Bugs. In any case, BEWARE RUGS!)

♥

Sometimes it took Lizzie a while to figure out how her mother's wisdom applied to her current situation. This was one of those times. She slid the cards back into their well-worn box, checked to see that no one was watching, and hugged it to her chest.

"I'm trying, Mother," she whispered. "I'm trying to be like you."

She crossed her eyes twice and made a wish that bandersnatches were just the beginning. That Wonderland *was* coming to her. All of it. And soon her mother would be there to pull Lizzie into her huge embrace and assure her she was doing all right.

CHAPTER 9

STORYBOOKER SHARE ⟨SLAM!⟩

W HEN CEDAR ARRIVED AT RAVEN AND
Apple's room, most of the other students
from her field trip were already seated on lounges
and chairs or on pillows on the floor, everyone arranged in a circle. Several dozen scented candles
burned, filling the room with the smell of baked
apple pie.

Lizzie Hearts entered beside her.

"Kind of a strange day, huh?" Cedar said.

"Strange days may be here to stay, and not to—"

Lizzie stopped suddenly and stared intensely at Cedar. "What rhymes with '*go away*'?"

Cedar shrugged and walked away. She rarely understood what Lizzie was talking about, but clearly she didn't want or need friends, let alone a chat with the puppet girl.

Raven was in urgent conversation with Apple, so Cedar sat on a couch beside Humphrey Dumpty and Poppy O'Hair.

"Hey," they said.

"Hey," said Cedar.

Cedar crossed her arms, trying to hide the bandersnatch teeth marks. She'd sand those off as soon as she got a chance.

"I love that color," said Poppy, indicating the sky-blue paint staining Cedar's fingertips, left over from a recent art project. "Art is one of my favorite subjects."

"Mine, too!" said Cedar. "I love painting."

"I'm into the verbal arts myself," said Humphrey. "I'll treat you to a little freestyle rap. Um…just give me a minute.…"

"I'm interested in sculpture," said Poppy. "Maybe

because my hands have so much practice styling hair. Do you like my new do?"

Poppy's hair grew royally fast, and she was always experimenting with new styles. Today it was a turquoise faux-hawk.

"Oh...well, it's kind of alarming," said Cedar.

Poppy blinked.

"Sorry!" said Cedar. "I didn't want to say that! I totally respect your individual style, even if I think you look like a bird built a nest on your head."

Poppy blinked twice. "Sorry!" said Cedar again.

"Got it!" Humphrey said. He began to rap, his extremely white hands gesturing in rapid motions.

Yo, Cedar and Poppy,
the talk's sounding choppy.
Don't wanna hop, T'
likes both of you guys,
so trade the lows for the highs,
say we stow the unwise.
Call a truce before war.
Let that snoozin' dog snore,
and opt for the choosin'
to not talk about hair, fair?

Humphrey smiled, as if certain he had just solved everything. Poppy looked confused, as if she wasn't sure whether to be upset.

"Sorry," Cedar whispered.

Apple stood at the head of the room and the talking quieted.

"Welcome, friends," said Apple. "Ever since Legacy Day, I have so enjoyed meeting together for our Storybooker Share Slams to discuss our Rebel situation—"

"And Royal," said Raven.

"…And Royal," said Apple, nodding. "But today we have even more serious matters to discuss."

"Yeah, what in Ever After was that play?" Sparrow said.

"That vas art!" said Helga Crumb, shaking her fist in the air.

"*Ja*, you are right, my cousin Helga," said Gus Crumb. "Headmaster Grimm is a genius!"

Apple cleared her throat. "I meant the appearance of the bandersnatches."

"Wait, did that play have anything to do with the bandersnatches?" asked Blondie, recording everything with her MirrorPad.

"Monsters appearing outside of their stories is the sort of catastrophe that happens when *people* don't follow their *destiny*," said Faybelle Thorn, glaring at Raven.

"I don't like it," said Nathan Nutcracker, sitting on the mantel. His jaw chattered, making a clicking sound. "I don't like it at all."

"A queen!" Lizzie shouted. "A queen is only as big as her fishbowl, so be careful not to behead too much of your water!"

Apple tilted her head, her lips pursed, as if trying very hard to take the statement seriously. "What do you mean, Lizzie?"

Lizzie slipped a card back into her pocket. "Ah...never mind. In context it doesn't really seem to apply."

"Why does *everything* have to go back to being a Royal or a Rebel?" Cerise said.

"Because these crazy, off-script things didn't use to happen before..." Apple glanced kindly at Raven.

"I don't see how my not signing the Storybook of Legends made bandersnatches appear on a mountaintop," said Raven.

"Well, I'll tell you one thing," said Faybelle. "It sure didn't help."

"Wait a splinter!" said Cedar, standing up. "Don't go blaming Raven. She was right to not sign."

Faybelle stood up, too, flipping her ponytail over her shoulder. "I don't get you, little Miss Pinocchio. Why are you a Rebel anyway? If I were you, I'd follow my script so I could get to the Happily Ever After and finally be *real*."

Nate Nutcracker gasped. Raven clenched her fists. Cedar met Faybelle's gaze.

"You're right, if I don't follow my destiny, I might be trapped in this wooden body forever—but even worse would be to be trapped in a choiceless life. If I can't lie, if I'm cursed to blurt out whatever I think even if I don't want to, then I can't *really* choose." She glanced at Poppy and then quickly away, afraid she might let slip another horrid opinion about her hair. "I think being a Rebel means you get to cut the strings and choose your story. And nothing is more important to me than choice."

"Hear! Hear!" said Maddie. "Though—and this isn't a criticism—I'd have enjoyed what you said more with a cup of tea." Maddie looked down at her hand, which was holding a cup of tea. "Oh! Well this is perfect now. Call off the hounds! Call off the king's men! I found my tea!"

"Rebel, Royal, bleh," said Kitty, examining her nails. "If you don't care where you want to end up, it doesn't matter which road you take."

"I don't know everything, but I know that choices are complicated," said Cedar. "Every choice we make affects other people. So if you're not sure where you want to end up, should you just hold still, choosing nothing?"

"Or should you leap ahead anyway," said Briar, "making bold choices and accepting where they take you?"

"And if they take you over a cliff?" asked Apple.

"If your destiny happens at the bottom of a cliff, then yes," said Briar.

"One should always know beforehand exactly what should happen, how it should happen, and then make it happen," said Lizzie.

"Look!" Cerise shouted, pointing.

A bunny was hopping up the face of Apple's grandfather clock. The clock chimed one, and the bunny ran down again. Cedar felt her mouth hang open. Such behavior wasn't uncommon for Ever After mice, but a bunny?

"Whoa," Dexter said, adjusting his glasses as if he couldn't believe what he'd just seen.

"Hickory dickory dock," Cerise whispered.

"Raven, did you do that?" Apple asked.

Raven shook her head. "I wouldn't even know what spell to use."

Cedar couldn't help saying aloud, "When the bunny reached the top, I swear it paused to check the time."

"What-ever-after," said Faybelle with an eye roll.

"Ha-ha!" said Lizzie, brandishing her scepter. "When is a mouse like a bunny?"

"Well," said Ashlynn kindly, "both are fluffy and cute and small and cute—"

"No," said Lizzie. She cleared her throat and looked at everyone significantly. "When is a mouse like a bunny? And when is a bear like a bandersnatch? Off-put? This is precisely my point!"

Cedar sighed. Lizzie's not making sense was the most normal thing about this day.

Apple wrangled the conversation back to bander-snatches and the headmaster's instructions to stay at the school, but Cedar kept her gaze on her hands, chipping off the blue paint. Perhaps if she managed not to notice anything, she might not blurt out something awkward and hurtful and lose any more friends.

CHAPTER 10

REASONABLE BY ACCIDENT ❓

WHEN APPLE DISMISSED THEM, LIZZIE WAS so full of thoughts she forgot to shout "Off with your head!" before leaving the room. Lizzie *knew* bunnies. She wouldn't exactly say she liked them—they were much too fluffy and softish and un-hedgehog-y—but she was royally *aware* of them. At no point had she sensed a bunny in Apple and Raven's room, despite the big-eared bouncer she'd seen with her eyes.

Lizzie's stately walk down the corridor nearly tripped into a skip. A giddy kind of excitement wiggled inside her, as if her stomach were a bag of popcorn in midpop. Bandersnatches! Jubjub birds! Bunnies that are obsessed with clocks! Were some of her subjects wriggling their way out of Wonderland and flocking to their princess? She took a deep breath and heard an extra inhale besides her own.

"It is unseemly to hide from your future queen," Lizzie said.

"Fine," said Kitty, slinking out of thin air. "Though I might have said 'un*seen*ly.'"

"What happened to that bunny rabbit?" Lizzie shouted.

"You mean the clock-climbing mouse that had somehow been transformed into a bunny?" said Kitty.

"Yes! Don't you *care* that you don't know how it happened? I would like to know, and am troubled by the fact that I do not!"

"Calm down, Princess Freak-Out." Kitty's smile weakened. "Now that you mention it, I'm *troubled*, too."

Unbeknownst to the Wonderlandians (except for Kitty, who can hear this narration right now but pretends not to), both Lizzie and Kitty had just used the word *troubled* for the first time in their lives.

"*Grrrr,*" Kitty growled.

Maddie was on her way to find a place that needed to be hopped on. But upon overhearing the Narrator mention things of a *troubling* nature, she hurried back down the hall to her fellow Wonderlandians.

"I'm concerned," said Maddie, and then immediately covered her mouth. "Oh no! It's happening to me, too!"

"What is?" Lizzie asked.

"I said I'm *concerned,*" Maddie said. "Not 'kilter-tipped' or 'taut-hearted' or even 'wormy-worried'! 'Concerned' is even worse than 'troubled'! It's Ever Afterlish! It's *boring,*" she whispered now, hand to the side of her mouth. "It's bland, heart-sapping plain-talk!"

Kitty shrugged. "It's not unlikely that enough time spent in a different place would introduce drift in your natural speech patterns." Kitty's eyes went wide, and then she, too, covered her mouth.

"See!" Maddie said, pointing at Kitty. "You said 'introduce drift—'"

Kitty interrupted. "Don't repeat it!"

"It," said Maddie.

"Not it," said Lizzie and Kitty in unison, and with that simple bit of madness, they realized all was not lost.

"That's a relief," Maddie said. "The Narrator just said we realized all was not lost. Now we need to find what actually *is* lost, and then everything will be fine again."

Lizzie wondered if something wasn't lost so much as found. Perhaps Wonderland had found her at last.

"Ooh, Lizzie, you think Wonderland is coming to Ever After?" Maddie asked.

"How did you know what I . . ." Lizzie started.

"The Narrator sometimes mentions what you're thinking."

"Nattering nosy nabob," Lizzie muttered. "Since you have no respect for royal privacy, tell us exactly what is going on, Nut-Bundled Know-It-All Narrator! Tell us why there are bandersnatches and jubjub birds and mice disguised in bunny-ness, and why Maddie is 'concerned' and Kitty is 'introducing drift'!"

No one said anything for a moment, except the Narrator, who didn't *say* anything, since this sentence was not audible to all parties.

"Did the Narrator tell you anything?" Lizzie asked.

"Nothing helpish or revealy," Maddie said. "It's a Narrator rule. They're not supposed to interact with the people in their story. Though you can trick them sometimes."

About that last part Maddie was completely wrong. At least with regards to this upstanding, rule-abiding Narrator.

"We need help," Lizzie said, stumbling over the words. She remembered one of her mother's cards:

♥

Worms NEED things. But a princess such as you ORDERS things. Today, put your things in order by ordering things to be what they are. And then, for fun, order them to be what they are not.

♥

Lizzie sighed. "We're having far too many reasonable thoughts to be able to figure out anything on our own."

"I'm sure Apple and Raven—" Maddie started to say, but Lizzie banged her scepter on the wall.

"They're reasonable even in the best of times! No, we need Wonder and riddles and sideways explanations. That's the kind of sense that will make sense of nonsense."

"I have a helpful suggestion," Maddie said. "But I'm afraid to say it because it might be *reasonable* by accident."

"Try saying it while standing on your head," Kitty suggested.

"Hat-tastic idea, Kitty!" Maddie bent over, balancing the rim of her teacup hat on the floor, and then flung her legs up into the air. "That's better. Anyway, we could go talk to Giles Grimm. The headmaster's brother? He lives in secret rooms beneath the library and only ever speaks in Riddlish."

Lizzie often visited the library, paging through books that reminded her of home—not because the books spoke or flew or read themselves backward, but because they had tales and pictures of Wonderland. It was nice to be reminded that she did have a home, a real home, a setting.

She followed Maddie and Kitty into the library,

through the stacks of books, out of the school entirely, past the sports fields, around a tree three times, back into the library, through a wall, down a narrow, dark, and properly eerie corridor, and into the Vault of Lost Tales.

"There wasn't a more direct route?" Lizzie asked.

"Probably," Maddie said, and gestured to the pile of rags sitting at a desk. "This is Giles. Hi, Giles!"

The pile of rags stood, and Lizzie realized it was a man wearing extremely raggedy clothes, so she thought she could be excused for mistaking him for refuse.

"Hello, er..." Lizzie said, searching her mind for an appropriate way to address the man, "Step-Headmaster Grimm."

Once upon a time, Giles Grimm had been co-headmaster, but Lizzie can also be forgiven for not knowing that.

"Party finds awkward twists in an unfound space made mist, lass," Giles said, smiling beneath his straggly gray beard.

"It does, indeed," Lizzie said, and then whispered to Maddie, "I'm not sure I caught all that. Usually

I'm quite conversant in Riddlish. Perhaps this wretched reasonability confounds my brain."

"Mine, too," Maddie said. "I'm not sure if it's the me-side or the he-side that has changed."

Giles nodded. "Wonders never cease. Just they find peace and pieces in creases. The bent land releases but queasy pieces, my Ms. Three nieces."

"Wonderland, you mean?" said Maddie. "Something about Wonderland?"

"When stare ye long into the face of bear become not bear but bandersnatch fair."

"He knows about the bandersnatches!" Lizzie said.

"Nay, fair is fare—though unfair—for the nightmare once cairned." Giles Grimm smiled kindly. "Don't forget the butter!"

"The butter?" Lizzie asked.

Giles nodded. "For the bandersnatch."

"Is this what it's like for the Ever Afterlings when they talk to us?" Lizzie asked. "Very frustrating."

"Maybe it would help if he stood on his head," Maddie whispered.

"Try this," Lizzie said. "Mr. Step-Headmaster Grimm, tell us, in the most unclear, confusing way you can imagine, whether or not things are changing."

Giles Grimm furrowed his brow as if thinking hard to come up with an incredibly difficult riddle. He cleared his throat, held up a finger, and said, "Yes."

"That was a silly question," Kitty whispered in Lizzie's ear. "We already *know* things are changing." Kitty disappeared and reappeared to whisper in her other ear. "What we need to know is *why* or *how*. And is there a cake or a pie in it for us? Lots of questions with more point and less silly were available."

Lizzie shrugged. "I didn't hear *you* speaking up with alternate questions, Catworm."

Maddie laughed. "It's catchy, right?"

Kitty did not appear to think it was catchy.

"Oh, Bookworm," Maddie said, presumably addressing the Narrator, though the Narrator had expressly expressed that Narrators must never be directly addressed.

Without warning, Giles Grimm vanished, and where he'd been standing a pile of books clattered to the floor.

"Oh, no, he disappeared!" Lizzie said. "Just when

I had a better question about whether or not to behead Kitty."

Kitty sniffed the books. "He didn't disappear. Disappearing things have a smell like the echo of a lemon. I think those books might actually *be* him."

"Oooh," Lizzie breathed out. Things changing into other things suddenly and without warning was a refreshing change of pace and slightly Wonderlandian. That giddy, popcorn-belly feeling returned.

Wonderland is coming to me....

A small nag caught in her thoughts. In Wonderland, Giles might have shrunk, or enlarged, or folded up on himself, but when things changed back home, they were still what they were. Not a person into a pile of books. That was magic, certainly, but was it the right kind? The wonderlandiful kind?

"Should I put the Grimmy books in my hat and take him with us?" Maddie asked.

"I wouldn't," Kitty said. "What if he turns back?"

"While stuck inside my hat?" Maddie said. "Good point."

"I didn't mean to make a good point," Kitty whined. "Making good points is not what I do!"

"Leave the book-man be," said Lizzie. "We'll

tell Headmaster Grimm about him when he gets back."

"*If* he gets back," Maddie said, and then coughed. "Sorry. Frog in my throat. *Ribbit.*"

Maddie stuck out her tongue, revealing a small blue frog perched upon it. The frog leaped off and hopped away. Maddie's eyes went wide.

Lizzie smiled. *Wonderland found me.*

CHAPTER 11

A WOBBLE OF UNCERTAINTY

EDAR WOOD WAS FEELING LIKE A HOLLOWED-
out log. Though she'd fled Raven's room the
moment the session ended, her unhappy encounter
with Poppy seemed to chase after her. Quick steps
down the corridor rattled her knee and elbow joints
with a jangle of metal and wood, but she didn't slow
down till she reached the safety of her dorm room.

Cedar opened her paint box. Black paint smeared
on her index finger and seemed to tingle, as if beck-
oning her to lose herself in her art. Cedar knew the
sensation was as false as everything else she felt. *If*

I were you, Faybelle had said, *I'd do anything to finally be real*. Perhaps Cedar was not a person at all but just a piece of wood who imagined she was a person.

She squeezed her creaky eyelids shut, trying to close off thoughts about wood and people and what she was or wasn't. Bits of sadness—imagined or not—were already worming into her heartwood. Maybe she could paint them away.

Today she set aside the traditional canvas and instead placed a wide wooden plank on her easel. She started to paint a scene of a garden early in the morning, when the colors were still hushed and full of grays, more shadow than not, shapes not yet fully revealed.

The paint couldn't completely hide the wood plank, its rough grain, lines, swirls, and knotholes as much a part of the picture as what she painted over them. It took some time before Cedar realized she was painting her own experience, bringing a kind of life to the dead wood but never changing what it was, never hiding it completely.

And that's what she loved about art. It spoke the unspeakable, revealed truth before the mind had a chance to think it.

It's not a real garden, Cedar thought, standing back to look at her painting, *but perhaps still worthwhile?*

From her pouch of art tools, she took out a knife to sharpen a quill she liked to use for making thin lines. The knife slipped and cut into her finger. That wasn't unusual. Cedar wasn't particularly careful.

But then a thin line of red welled up along the cut. At first, she thought it was paint, but it grew. A red bead, fat as a honeybee, bled out and dropped from her finger, splashing onto the purple carpet. Cedar felt—truly *felt*—a sensation she had never experienced before: a slicing, hot, sharp fierceness, a hugeness as big as life trapped in the tip of her finger. She whispered the word: "Pain."

Cedar Wood's finger was bleeding.

She shouted toward Cerise Hood's side of their dorm room, "Look! Look, my finger is bleeding!"

But Cerise wasn't there. Cedar examined her fingertip again. It felt softer than normal. She patted herself, her hands bumping against the brass pegs at her joints. She traced the knot of wood that marked her left thigh like an oval birthmark. Still there. And yet, when she lifted her finger to her mouth to suck on it, she tasted blood—salty and metallic and warm. Not just imagined the taste. Really tasted it. Like the difference between looking at a photo of a beach and actually putting bare feet in the sand.

Cedar giggled and performed a short dance that was a burst of joy, a wobble of uncertainty, and a flinch of fear all at the same time. Was something marvelous happening? Or something scary?

The bubble and rush of emotions made it impossible to stay still. Cedar ran out the door and down the hall.

"Help? I think?" Cedar called out. "Or maybe hooray? I'm not sure, but one of the two!"

No one answered.

She knocked on Maddie's door, finding it open but no one inside. No one except Maddie's pet dormouse, Earl Grey, who was standing on Maddie's tea table squeaking and strutting about. As Cedar drew closer, she could see he was wearing a dashing black silk shirt and trousers and holding up a tiny skull in one hand.

"*Squeak squeak, squ-squeak squeak squeak?*" he squeaked.

It appeared that Earl Grey was practicing a dramatic scene from *Hamlet*.

"Earl Grey?" Cedar said.

Earl Grey startled, dropped the skull, and leaned nonchalantly against a teacup as if he'd been just hanging out and not rehearsing his one-mouse show at all.

"Do you know where Maddie is?" Cedar asked.

Earl Grey shrugged, put back on his top hat, and leaped onto Cedar's shoulder, eager to go with her to track Maddie down.

Across the hall, Gus and Helga's door was ajar. Cedar couldn't see them inside, but two heaps of breadcrumbs sat in the middle of their rug.

"Hello?" said Cedar.

Another new sensation crawled over her—a ticklish, cold, worrying sort of thing, like thousands of icy fingernails skipping down her limbs. Chills. Cedar had imagined chills before, but her imagination had failed to create the combination of pleasure and discomfort, the shudder and exhale.

Beneath her, the floor rolled as if the castle had started to gallop and then changed its mind. Cedar shook her head. Perhaps she was sick. Could she have contracted some rare wood disease that was causing her magic-enlarged imagination to overreact?

Out the window, Cedar spotted several small shapes dropping from the roof. Above the Crumbs' room was Ashlynn's balcony, and Cedar knew songbirds often congregated there. Had the songbirds been hurt and fallen? Cedar raced to the window but spotted no injured songbirds in the courtyard below, only a flock of dodoes, those odd-looking flightless birds, lurching around as if bewildered.

"I know how you feel," Cedar said.

"*Squeak*," said Earl Grey.

Cedar ran to Raven and Apple's room. Raven had magical abilities, and whatever was happening just had to be magic.

As she raced up the stairs, again the castle seemed to burp, the stairs swaying under her feet. The warm stab in her fingertip traveled down her arm and into her chest, where it flared to a pain that was as sweet as it was agonizing. The pain left behind a strange and wondrous thumping as if something were moving inside her chest. Moving, like the waves of the ocean. The beating of a drum. The buzzing of a dragonfly's wings. The rolling meters of a song. The *everything* of the world caught and moving inside her chest.

Cedar ran harder, as if she could somehow catch up to whatever wondrousness was happening to her and seize it, hold on to it, and make it hers forever.

And Cedar ran even harder, as though she could somehow flee the frightening changes altering her body.

As she leaped onto the next floor, she heard several small, heavy things fall off her and bounce down the stairs. She didn't turn to see what she'd left behind, her body in agony to be running so hard and yet burning with exquisite joy. She burst through Raven's door.

"Raven!" she shouted. "Something's—"

But she didn't have to tell Raven that strangeness had erupted at Ever After High.

Apple was standing before a mirror, a gasp of horror escaping her throat. Raven's hands were covering her mouth.

Apple turned as Cedar entered. The light from the window fell on Apple's face, revealing a deep red coloring her round cheeks and moving outward to paint her whole face. Sticking out of the top of her head was a finger-sized piece of wood. Even as Cedar stared, a lime-green leaf sprouted from the stick and unfurled itself to face the sunlight. It was a stem.

Raven pointed at Cedar in shock and opened her mouth as if to speak, but no sound came out.

Cedar hugged her arms around her chest. She felt warmth, softness, aliveness. The brass pegs at her elbows and wrists were gone. She touched her knees—gone there, too. Those were what had dropped away on the stairs.

She dared to turn to a mirror. Her hair looked as it always had—warm brown, wavy, and heavy as frayed rope. Her dress was the same lavender and coral one she'd put on that morning. But if not for those details, she might have assumed she was looking at a stranger. Her dark brown limbs and face were smooth, no wood grain, no chipped spots where she'd bumped into something (like bandersnatch teeth). She blinked, and her eyes were wet. Two tears freed themselves from her lashes and rolled down her cheeks, leaving behind a cold, ticklish path.

She inhaled sharply for the first time, and she felt her chest—her lungs?—fill up, pressing against that constant winged, wave-ish, drumlike beating of a...a...a *heart*.

Her heart.

Her real heart beating in her chest.

She pressed her hands against the beating, crying faster with wonder and alarm and joy, so filled with the music of her aliveness she feared she might explode.

"Raven, what's happening?" Cedar whispered.

But the only response was a single, frightened squawk.

CHAPTER 12

~~WONDERLAND FOUND ME~~

Eat More Muffins!

IZZIE, KITTY, AND MADDIE WALKED OUT of the library, sounds wafting over their heads like invisible birds. *Suss-suss. Hiss-hoo. Waaaahhh.* Lizzie wondered if she was hearing the books whisper to each other. Or if the air itself had come alive.

The cushioned chairs in the hall just outside the library door were huddled together as though in conversation. When the girls neared, they scattered, their short wooden forelegs making clumping noises like little hooves.

Lizzie felt so good she longed for a ripping game of croquet. She pretended her scepter was a flamingo mallet, lined it up, and swung at an imaginary hedgehog.

"Things are obviously changing," Lizzie said.

"See?" Kitty said. "It was a pointless question."

The rug beneath Lizzie's feet rippled. Remembering her mother's advice to avoid rugs, Lizzie stepped off, just as a tasseled end flicked to where her feet had been.

Outside the window, a stone gargoyle carved into the school's facade flapped its wings. And then the window Lizzie was looking through blinked. Startled, she took a step back.

"Well, I never!" said Lizzie. It seemed bad-mannered to blink when someone was actively looking through you.

"This is Wonder-smacking awesome!" Maddie shouted.

Wonderland coming to find me.

Lizzie smiled so hard she felt like Kitty. Her adopted world was becoming what she, Lizzie Hearts, needed it to be! Perhaps soon all parts of Ever After would smell and feel and sound as perfectly extraordinary and Wondery as the Grove. Perhaps now she would not have to spend all her energy just trying to hide her homesickness.

But first, she would need to teach the new world some manners, blinking windows and such. Her mother would certainly expect this. There would be much Ruling and Ordering and Shaping Things Up.

Maddie cocked her head to one side. "This is a slice of strange pie. Why don't we hear any screaming or whining or what's-going-on-ing? Chair herds and window blinks are just the kind of world-spin that leaves the Ever Afterlings...well, *troubled*."

"Perhaps they've finally come away from their senses," said Lizzie.

"Maybe," Maddie said. "Hey, Narrator, what are Raven and Apple doing?"

Maddie waited, eyebrows raised, mistakenly expecting the Narrator to break the rules and interact with her.

"Hmm, when the Narrator is being this secretsy and rule-ish, that means there's something Big and Important happening that the Narrator is trying very hard not to reveal," said Maddie.

It does not!

"So we should probably go check on Raven and Apple," said Maddie. "Tell them what's up."

"Do we know what's up?" Kitty asked.

"Well, we should act like it, even if we don't," Lizzie proclaimed. "Own the up!"

This was a quote from one of her mother's cards:

♥

Whether up or down, inside or out, it is yours.
Own the down. Own the up.

♥

The girls made their way past another group of chairs chatting in an incomprehensible furniture language.

"What do you suppose they even have to talk about?" Lizzie asked. "It's not like the life of furniture is particularly interesting."

"Maybe they're discussing ways to make life more interesting," Kitty whispered.

The thought made Lizzie shiver.

She shook the shivers away. She would simply order the chairs to behave! If Wonderland was indeed coming to Ever After, Lizzie had no time to waste. She must be as queenly as her mother would be.

The door to the dorms didn't look alive like a chair or blinky like a window, but when the three girls walked through, it made a disconcerting gulping noise.

"Ew," Kitty said. "I feel like we've just been swallowed."

"Halloo, friends," Maddie shouted, entering Raven and Apple's room. "Oh, nobody's here."

"Nobody's anywhere, it seems," Kitty purred.

The school was unusually empty today, and they hadn't seen *anyone* since leaving the library. Anyone human, anyway.

"Our story appears to be a series of Looking Glass adventures without the glass," Kitty said.

A little noise uncurled from deep within the room, like the whimpering of a pat of butter cornered by a piece of toast. Lizzie did not hear it, Kitty chose to ignore it, and Maddie uncharacteristically assumed Apple and Raven's room wouldn't contain anything like talking butter or aggressively warm toast.

"Wait!" Maddie said, questioning her assumptions after hearing what the Narrator had said. "There *is* someone in here."

"We should get out of this school and find one of the teachers," said Lizzie.

"Frighteningly sensible, Lizzie," Kitty said.

Lizzie frowned. "You're right. What is the matter with me?"

"Hello?" Maddie called out.

A tuft of dark hair popped up from behind a writing desk, followed by two brown eyes. "Maddie?" said a mouth, conceivably somewhere below the eyes.

"Cedar!" Maddie called, running to the girl and pulling her out and into a big hug. "You're all meaty! How did that happen? And you're shivering. Are you cold? No? Oh, scared, right. You came looking for Apple and Raven, too, didn't you? But they've disappeared, just like Giles Grimm!"

"*Not* disappeared, just like Giles Grimm," Kitty said, sniffing the room.

"They...they—" Cedar started, when a black bird perched on the writing desk squawked.

"Crow!" Lizzie shouted, pointing at the bird as if accusing it of something.

"*Raven*," Cedar whispered, and then pointed at a plump red apple on the floor. "And Apple."

"Oooh!" Lizzie said with a little laugh. "Delicious!"

Cedar's eyes widened in further shock.

"Not literally, I mean," Lizzie muttered. "Who eats raw ravens anymore? And that apple, especially knowing it's an Apple-apple, is bound to be much too sweet. And full of organs. Note to everyone—don't eat that apple. It's probably gross."

The toilet flushed from inside the bathroom. The door opened, and a squat little crocodile about the height of Maddie walked out on its stubby hind legs. It carried a newspaper under one arm.

"Mornin', ladies," it said, dropping to all fours. "Feelin' a bit peckish, what."

"Peckish?" Lizzie asked, always willing to have a conversation with a crocodile. "Like, birdy?"

"Like 'ungry." The crocodile was marching toward the Apple-apple.

The Raven-raven began dive-bombing the crocodile.

"*Oy*," the crocodile shouted, swinging its head around. "Jus' tryin' a get breakfast, soddin' bird!"

Maddie picked up the Apple-apple and put it safely in her hat. "C'mon, Raven," she said, running for the door. "Let's leave Mr. Hungry Teeth on his own."

"*Aaaaaah*," the crocodile bellowed, running at the lot of them. Lizzie stared at the teeth. They were fascinating. So many of them. She could do a lot with teeth like that. The teeth kept getting closer until suddenly the raven pecked her on the forehead.

"How dare you!" Lizzie shouted, and only then realized she might be on the crocodile's menu. She took quick steps out the door, Cedar slamming it shut behind her.

"Where did that crocodile even come from?" Cedar asked, panting.

"Probably from the toilet," Maddie said. "There's loads of them in the sewers, you know."

"That's alligators," Kitty said.

"Oh, right," said Maddie. "Alligators. I don't know about that crocodile, then."

A deep bass rumbling shook the floor, as if the world were beginning to turn in exactly the opposite direction as the building it supported. *More changes?* Lizzie rubbed her hands together.

Cedar jumped away from the closed door. "Is that creature getting through?"

"Be reasonable. Crocodiles don't have the thumbs necessary to open doors," said Lizzie.

"It could be *eating* its way through," Kitty said.

Cedar eyed the door nervously.

"Something is happening out on the terrace, though," Lizzie said. "A crowd is gathering. A queen can tell these things."

"You're not a queen *yet*," Cedar whispered.

"If I say I am, I am!" Lizzie shouted as she marched downstairs. "It is a queen's prerogative to determine reality."

"What's a prerogative?" Maddie asked.

Lizzie ignored Maddie's question, partly because she wasn't actually sure what a prerogative was. But most of her was riddled and ant-dance-y with the worry that she might be lying to herself and the others about being ready to be a queen.

♥

*A queen worrying about others is like a baker
worried he's making too many muffins.
As if there could be such a thing as
Too Many Muffins. Ha! WORRY NOT!
AND EAT MORE MUFFINS!*

♥

But I can't help worrying, Mother, Lizzie wanted to
say. She had yet to read a card that explained how
her mother lived worry-free.

Lizzie clenched her teeth and marched toward
the crowd-feeling on the terrace. And the parts of
her that weren't wormy with worry or puzzled with
prerogative began to pulse with excitement.

Wonderland found me!

The sunshine seemed especially bright, warming
her gold crown against her forehead. On the terrace, a podium faced rows of chairs as if set up for
an event like Legacy Day. Or a coronation. Her
coronation?

Lizzie lifted her nose, tightened her lips, pressed
one hand against the worry in her belly, pressed the
other hand against the eager beats of her heart, and
smiled.

"These chairs weren't here when we came back from the field trip," Cedar said.

"Maybe the people setting this up were the crowd we heard," Maddie said. "The faculty must be back! Yay!"

At Maddie's shout, all the chairs turned and *looked* at them.

"Uh-oh," said Kitty.

"The chairs set themselves up," Cedar whispered. "What I want to know is, what was the podium telling them to do?"

An incomprehensible noise, somewhere between a shout, the crackle of a fire, and a bone breaking, issued from the podium.

The chairs nodded. And then they began to charge.

Lizzie's stomach dropped. This was not her coronation. This was some kind of uprising.

"*Run!*" Lizzie yelled.

And they did.

"They're not very fast," Kitty said, running backward.

"What are you talking about?" Lizzie shouted, casting a glance over her shoulder. "They're gaining on us!"

Kitty shrugged, disappeared, and then reappeared, running a few feet in front of the group. "We're not very fast either."

"I can't...keep...this up," Cedar gasped. "Not really...used to...breathing...like this...or at all...."

Maddie held her hand.

The girls zoomed through corridor after corridor, past flighty curtains, over grumbly carpets, around mischievous benches. But the charging chairs stayed on their heels, the podium thump-hopping in front, shrieking microphone feedback that sounded like a battle cry.

"Maybe the chairs...are mad...that we've been sitting on them...all these years," Maddie said between huffs and puffs.

"This...is...*not*...wonderlandiful," Lizzie said.

Ahead, nearly blocking the hall, was what appeared to be a garden shed.

"Hutling!" Maddie yelled.

On hearing its name, the small cottage stood up on two chicken legs and turned to them "face"-first. There was a door. Mouth. Whatever. Only a couple of weeks ago, this offspring of Baba Yaga's magic hut had hatched from its egg, but already it'd grown so much that when it was standing, the doorknob was too high for Maddie to reach. And the stampede of seats had caught up.

With a tremendous clacking and whacking, armchairs, easy chairs, folding chairs, and stools galloped closer. The hutling made a distressed clucking sound. It took a few steps forward, bringing the four girls underneath its shadow, like baby chicks under their mother.

"Is it going to squish us?" Cedar asked.

"The hutling is my buddy! We play hide-and-seek all the time," Maddie whispered, "Don't tell, but I trick the hut every time by hiding inside it." Maddie snickered.

The crowd of chairs had stopped before the hutling, confused, turning back and forth.

"Can't they see us?" Cedar whispered. "We're right in front of them."

"Of course they can't," Lizzie said, sure she was right. Or pretending to be sure. She wasn't entirely sure of the difference at this point.

The hutling started to walk away.

"Stay with it!" Lizzie said, shuffling to keep up.

Kitty's ears pricked up. "Did you hear that? Like breaking glass, but…windier."

"Breaking wind?" Maddie asked, giggling.

"Wind and broken glass? It couldn't be a…a *shardstorm*," Cedar whispered.

Lizzie had only heard fables about shardstorms— the frightening weather events that occurred when a great deal of magic mirrors broke all at once. Surely they were as imaginary as polka-dotted unicorns, as flying mushrooms, as hideous bunnies. Nobody ever saw them, because they were supposed to fade or collapse as soon as they were confronted with their own reflection, and reflections were everywhere in Ever After. Yet who knew what was possible in this change-up, mess-around, come-undone school?

The ringing and crackling and tinkling and whooshing grew louder. And louder. The air began to buzz, the sound of ten thousand clocks striking midnight at the same time.

"Shardstorm!" Lizzie yelled. *"Run!"*

CHAPTER 13

TRAPPED!

HE GRIMMNASIUM DOOR THRUST OPEN.

"Quick! Come inside!" shouted a haggard, but still dashing, Daring Charming.

The sound of breaking glass raged behind them. The Raven-raven soared through the open doorway of the Grimmnasium after the hutling. Cedar was about to follow but was struck from the side. A folding chair pounced on top of her, folding and unfolding its seat menacingly. About to kick the thing off, Cedar felt herself pale (for real) at the sight behind the chair.

A tornado of mirror glass the size of a mature oak tree rounded the corner and spun down the hall. It was beautiful, the way the light reflected off each individual piece of sharpened glass, and Cedar found herself wondering what colors of paint she'd use to create the scene on canvas.

The chair leaped off her and charged the storm. And was instantly shredded to bits.

Lizzie shook her fist at the disintegrated chair. "That will teach you to unceremoniously tackle the personal acquaintance of a royal heir to Wond—"

"Come on!" Maddie said, pulling Cedar and Lizzie inside the Grimmnasium. Glass shards began pelting the metal doors just as Daring slammed them shut.

He turned to the girls with a brilliant smile, leaning against the door casually as if not one bit worried about the screaming shardstorm pelting the other side of the door.

"Good afternoon, ladies," Daring said. "A pleasure to save you."

Lizzie rolled her eyes.

"Can it get through that door?" Cedar asked.

Daring gave the door a hard slap. "Dwarven metal. Tough stuff."

Cedar was shivering from her noncreaky toes to her soft shoulders, her new, real body confused by new, real bruises forming from that rogue chair attack. She found herself wondering if maybe there was a way to bypass being regular skin *or* wood, and get turned into dwarven metal instead.

"But I don't think I've had the pleasure, enchanting lady." Daring kissed the back of Cedar's hand. She felt the warmth of his lips, and mothergoosebumps scattered across her arm. "New here? I'm Daring Charming, but the girls just call me Prince Daring Charming."

He winked.

Lizzie rolled her eyes again. Cedar wanted to roll her eyes, too. After all, she'd never been one to bat her eyelashes at Daring or sigh whenever he slew dragons or lifted heavy objects or buttered his bread in muscle-flexing, manly motions. Still, she'd never felt the needle-thin tap dance of mother-goosebumps across real skin. She'd never experienced this warm, pleasant rumble in her belly and dizzy, tingling confusion in her head. If a simple kiss on the hand from Daring Charming could produce such sensations, what would her whole life be like now that she was real? Maybe she didn't want to be wood—or dwarven metal. Despite pain and fear, realness had some charming perks.

"That's Cedar, you gooseberry brain," said Lizzie. "She changed."

"She's not the only one," said Daring, gesturing.

The Grimmnasium was a huge open room with glossy hardwood floors, bleachers, a basketball court in the center, and a running track around the edges. Today it seemed darker than normal, and unfamiliar, un-sporty objects cluttered everywhere.

"What a mess," Lizzie said, adjusting her black gloves as if longing to get to work.

"Hunter, Dexter, and I were practicing tower-climbing when the changes started," said Daring. "So we gathered all the students we could find to take refuge here. Rescuing those in distress—that's what I do."

He winked at Cedar again.

Daring began pointing out inanimate objects that

had been their classmates: a pair of crystalline shoes that had been Ashlynn Ella, a heart-shaped layer cake that had been Cupid. As his arm extended, Cedar noticed a light sheen of gray fur covering Daring's skin.

"You've aged a great deal since I saw you last, Charming," Lizzie said. "Gray before your time, though perhaps not yet strangled by an octopus."

Daring looked at the backs of his hands and laughed nervously. "Yeah. Everyone was fine when we came in here. I mean, Hunter had leaves for hair, and a rose was blooming behind Briar's ear, but . . . then things got worse."

Cedar noticed a small tree growing out of the floor. There was an ax tangled in its leaves, and its branches arched protectively over the crystal shoes. Behind it, a pink rosebush grew up one wall.

"Oh, no," Cedar said.

"At least Ashlynn wasn't turned into hot cinders," Kitty said, testing a shoe's size with her own foot. "That would be very awkward for flammable Huntsman the Tree here."

A golden lock and a large brass egg lying by Cedar's feet were surely Blondie and Humphrey.

Cedar could sense a blister forming on her foot, but the rest of the students seemed to have changed in the opposite direction from her—less real, less human.

A wolf cub with bright red fur dashed across the Grimmnasium and rubbed her head against Cedar's ankles.

"Cerise?" Cedar asked.

The cub wagged her tail and ran off.

An enormous black-and-white-checkered cygnet shedding loose feathers and squawking had to be Duchess.

A sleigh bell with fairy wings awkwardly flitted past Cedar, clanging mournfully.

"Faybelle?" Cedar asked, and the bell rang.

The lights in the Grimmnasium began to flash. Once, twice, three times. Then every mirror in the room flickered, and Milton Grimm's face appeared in them.

"Students!" said the headmaster. "I am using our emergency broadcast system to broadcast a state of emergency. Ever After High has been infected with a wild magic. Madam Baba Yaga has conducted a magical analysis and believes the cause is...is...

well, is quite distressing, so please prepare your-selves. We believe the Jabberwock has returned."

Cedar gasped. The inanimate objects in the room rustled. The Raven-raven squawked and flapped around in circles.

"Baba Yaga is even now preparing a magical bar-rier that will completely enclose the school grounds in order to contain the Jabberwock's infection. If you are still able, please exit the grounds immedi-ately. In fifteen minutes, the barrier will go up, and anyone inside the school will be quarantined until we resolve the issue. Thank you."

"Quarantined?" Daring asked.

"He means trapped," Kitty said, her hair gaining a bit more volume than usual. Her constant smile seemed absolutely terrified. "They're going to trap us in here! Till they contain the...the infection."

"Wait...the Jabberwock's infection?" said Cedar. "That beast is what's changing everything in here? So...is *it* in the school, too?"

Kitty squeaked and popped out of sight.

The image of a clock replaced Grimm's face. One hand pointed at the number three, and the second hand of the clock began to spin backward.

"Off with our heads!" Lizzie yelled.

Daring drew his sword and then paused. "Wait. What?" he asked.

Lizzie cleared her throat. "I mean, let's move! We've got to get out of here! Everyone, grab as many students as you can and run!"

Daring nodded, sheathed his sword, and promptly disappeared.

"Enough disappearing!" Lizzie yelled, stamping her foot. "I have had it with the sudden disappearing!"

"Again, not disappeared," Kitty said, reappearing. She nodded downward.

A furry creature the height of Lizzie's knee stood with paws on hips, its sharp teeth bright white as if recently bleached. It was the cutest little beastie Cedar had ever seen, with wide eyes and tiny horns, wearing perfectly tailored mini-replicas of Daring's clothing. It let out a squeaky roar.

"Right," Lizzie said. "Daring-beastie, can you carry Blondie?"

"*Rrryes,*" the little beast growled, and scampered over to the golden lock.

Cedar picked up the Cupid cake and examined the

Briar rosebush to see if there was any way to safely uproot it. She glanced at the countdown clock. One minute had already passed. She blinked and looked again. The second hand on the clock was spinning faster and faster.

"We're not going to make it!" she yelled.

"The hutling can carry us," said Maddie. "It's a good runner, and I'm sure it wants to get out, too."

The hutling bobbed its roof, and its front door swung open.

Lizzie flung the Faybelle bell into the hut with a clang and clambered through the door.

Kitty clomped closer, wearing the Ashlynn shoes. "Tell me how going in there doesn't count as that thing eating us."

"Hutling is nice!" Maddie said, dropping Earl Grey onto her hat and pocketing the Humphrey egg before hoisting herself through the door. "It only eats wood and things like that."

Cedar instinctively cringed, but then remembered she wasn't wooden anymore. "Here are Cupid and Cerise," she said, dropping off the cake and wolf cub. "But what about the others?... Hunter and Briar..."

The clock hand spun faster, filling the room with a buzzing sound.

"A tree and a rosebush won't fit in here." Lizzie grabbed Cedar's arm and pulled her into the hut, the door slamming shut behind her.

The inside looked exactly like that of a small one-room cottage, complete with a tiny couch and chair, table, and fireplace, so cramped even Maddie couldn't stand upright. Cedar crouch-ran to one of the tiny windows.

The Daring beastie was standing protectively in front of the Briar rosebush. He was gesturing frantically.

"Daring is still out there!" Cedar yelled.

The window she was looking through swung open even as the hut began to run. The little Daring monster closed one eye as if aiming, pulled back his arm, and hurled the golden lock straight through the open window, missing Cedar by an inch. The window slammed shut, and Cedar caught a glimpse of a fuzzy Daring giving her a thumbs-up before the hutling ran out of the Grimmnasium at top speed.

"Run, hut-beast!" Lizzie yelled. "Take us beyond the grounds of Ever After High!"

Just then, the timer thundered through the school, sounding like a cuckoo clock in a great deal of pain.

CUCKOO! CUCKOOOO! CUCKOOOOOOOO!

"No way that was fifteen minutes!" said Cedar.

"Bah. Outside the school, it might have been," said Lizzie. "Sometimes in Wonderland, time moves sideways."

"No, no, we have to get out," Cedar said.

The hutling had pushed its way past the broken chairs outside the Grimmnasium door and was jogging through the corridor. There was a loud frizzle and a hiss, and through the window Cedar could see the sky outside turn a deep yellow, the color of Baba Yaga's magic. The magic barrier was up.

"We're trapped," said Cedar. "We need to...to...get help! Find some teachers or adults, perhaps a helpful woodsman or fairy godmother, maybe a wise old crone who turns out to be a good witch after we share some bread with her—"

"We don't have any bread," said Kitty.

"I have a butter knife!" Lizzie said brightly.

"You know what I mean!" Cedar yelled. Her heart was pounding, her skin felt thin as paper, and she couldn't seem to catch her breath. "In the stories, the brave young girls with pure hearts always get help from some wise adult person, and we need to find that wise adult person immediately!"

Kitty peered out a window. "Calm down, freaker-hosen. This doesn't look like any story I've read before."

Cedar *was* freaking out. Old Cedar might get sad and quiet and lonely, but shout frantically at her friends? Maybe changing into a real girl had made her loopy.

"We must help ourselves," said Lizzie. "I am the daughter of the Queen of Hearts. I will simply rule this unruly land and squeeze it into my control. It's already half Wonderland. Perhaps all it needs is a monarch."

Cedar detected a slight quaver in Lizzie's voice. Lizzie was always in control, wasn't she? Always sure she *could be* in control, anyway, even if she wasn't. Cedar took several deep breaths. This whole breathing thing was new to her, but she was finding that doing it deep and slow was much more calming than shallow and fast.

"They *have* to let us out." She pulled her Mirror-Phone from her pocket to call the headmaster or her father. "No! It says 'out of area.' I always get a signal in the school. How can it be out of area?"

"Our areas have slipped and nipped," said Kitty. "Everything is upside down and sideways, except what's inside out. There may also be a cherry on top."

"You guys have to fix this!" said Cedar. "Everyone changed but you. The Jabberwock is trying to magic Ever After into Wonderland, but you're already Wonderlandian, so its magic doesn't affect you, right? You're immune?"

"It has changed us a little," said Maddie. "I mean, don't you all feel a little more...reasonable?"

"Being more reasonable is a good thing," Cedar said, still tapping at her MirrorPhone just in case it would suddenly work.

"Flesh puppet," Lizzie said, straightening the small curtains on the window that had allowed the Blondie lock entrance, "we are inside a cottage walking around on chicken legs. What use is reason right now?"

Lizzie bustled about nervously, tidying up the cottage, setting Faybelle upright, straightening chairs. It was like she was playing house. It didn't seem to matter to her that nothing made sense, only that it was out of order.

"You're always talking about order. So put it in order!" Cedar pointed at the window. Several winged cheeses flew by.

Lizzie glared at Cedar icily and opened her mouth to surely express the certain knowledge that A FOX PLUGGED THE FENCE.

Maddie stopped stOCK-STILL. A QUILL SPILLED ILL TRILLS.

"Oh, no," said Maddie.

"Not good," said Kitty.

A FROG SQUIRRELED TWICE AND BACKED UP.

"What's not good?" asked Cedar. "What's wrong now?"

"Nothing, surely. Right? Keep the hutling moving," Lizzie said, but worry striPED ALONG THE RIVER.

"Narrator?" said Maddie. "You're just teasing us with the jibber and jabber, right?"

It was clear that something was indeed GA-LUMPHING, but with a certain SPECIFIC SOCK, THERE WOULD BE A DOG.

"The narration has gone wonky," Maddie saNDWICHED. "Maybe the Jabberwock's magic affects everyone—even our Narrator!"

CHAPTER 14

THE NARRATOR TAKES A SICK DAY

Wait...what?

Um, Narrator? Narrator, are you okay?

Please don't interrupt, Maddie. Everything is happening so rapidly I need complete concentration to observe and describe the FIDDLE-PIE-MY, OH THERE SHE GOES, WEEEE!

The, uh, the fiddle-pie-my? Narrator, do you speak Riddlish? Hat-tastic! But I couldn't quite translate it. What was that second part again?

I'm not speaking Riddlish. What I'm trying to say is this is a situation of UTMOST ROAST BEEF, and if I don't CACKLE TACKLE FINGER IN MY EYE, KNOCKS AT THE DOOR, A CHICKEN IN DISGUISE?

While the idea of "utmost roast beef" seems perfectly lovely, and I am hextremely fond of the odd thing, the oddness in your speaking is making me a little nervous.

Oh dear. Maddie, something *is* wrong with me. I can hear it now. I'm trying to tell the story, but HUMPTY LUMPTY OATMEAL WITH RAISINS! Oh no! I'm SPICY BUTTERED NOODLES! I'm LOBSTER SAUCE!

No! Narrator, the magic just can't change you, too! If you can't tell the story, then it stops right here, skipping over the climax and resolution straight to The End, and Raven's still a raven and Apple's still an apple and Ever After High is jabberwocked forever after with no hope of undoing the doneness! Please, Narrator, you have to keep narrating! Please!

SPINACH BETWEEN MY TOES!

Narrator?

SAND IN THE SANDWICH, MY, WHAT A CRUNCHY LUNCH!

Okay. It's going to be okay. I am the daughter of the Mad Hatter. I must put on my thinking cap and figure this out. Let's see, I'm sure I have a thinking cap in my Hat of Many Things...ah-ha! Here it is, hiding under Apple-apple. Well, the cap fits a little snug, but it'll do. So think. No matter what, the story must go on. I read that in the Narration hextbook I borrowed from the library. And in order for a story to go on, it must have a Narrator. So if our Narrator is unable to fulfill the narration duties, we simply find an alternate Narrator. Someone who is untouched by the mystery-making magic. Which would mean a Wonderlandian. Perhaps someone who understands the basics of narration because she has been eavesdropping on Narrators her whole life. But…who could that be?

SQUIGGLE THE TIMES!

I don't know what you're saying! You're not speaking Riddlish, and you're not speaking a riddle. Help me, Narrator, please! Who can narrate us through this story?

A DANCE OF SPOONS, STIRRING CLOUDS OF MILK.

I wish I could figure out what you're saying. But with this tiny thinking cap on, all I can think about is the tightness around my brow. And that makes me think of my own head. And that makes me think of me. Me. Me?

Yes, already! You! There's no one else!

Really, Kitty? You think I should narrate the story? That seems like a hero's job, something Raven or Apple would do to save the day. But I'm a Hatter. I have read about different types of characters in a narration book, and I'm clearly the quirky best friend or the comic relief. I'm the helper, not the doer. I'm definitely not the hero!

CINDERS AND ELEPHANT PIE. *CINDERS AND ELEPHANT PIE!*

Okay. Okay. I'm the Narrator.

CHAPTER 15

SWAMP JUICE IN YOUR TEACUP

ADDIE? WHAT THE TIMBERSTICKS IS going on?"

"Uncertain how to proceed, Madeline Hatter began to speak, she said."

"Um, Maddie, what are you talking about?"

"All the girls were staring at her like Madeline had just eaten an entire gooseberry pie with her nose, she said."

"Did Maddie get hit on the head?"

"I don't think so, but I am always willing to give head-bonking a try. Fetch me a flamingo!"

"Maddie shook her head to clear cobwebs and tried to figure out this narration thing without talking, um, she said.... I mean, Maddie said. Wait. Am I supposed to say that out loud?"

"I'm confused."

"You aren't the only one, Cedar Scratchingpost."

"Oh dear, I'm really making a mess of this," said Maddie.

"Wait!" said Kitty. "Do that. You *narrated* 'said Maddie' instead of saying it aloud. That was more like how the Narrator does it."

"This is truly troubling," Cedar said, looking around nervously.

"That, too!" Kitty said, getting unusually excited. "Exactly! You noticed that I'm unusually excited, and you narrated that information. Wait... how did you do that? I can't normally hear your thoughts."

"I'm trying out something new," Maddie said. "I'm not just thinking about what's going on—I'm *narrating* it. It's different from talking and different from normal thinking. It's thinking *out loud*."

"But how?" said Kitty. "That's amazing, I wonder if—no, I don't wonder anything. I am Kitty Cheshire and I do not get involved. What's the matter with me? Shutting up now—cat's got my tongue and all that."

"What in the blighted name of bunnies is going on?" Lizzie shouted. "Tell me at once!"

"The Narrator is sick," Maddie said.

"*Sick?*" Lizzie bellowed. "How can a bodiless thing one barely believes exists be sick? And why do I apparently care?"

"The Jabberwock's magic is transforming our Narrator, too," Maddie said.

"Without a Narrator, the story would end," Cedar said, her eyebrows up high as if trying to make room for all the thoughts filling her head. "We would stay here, trapped inside a school that is all hexed up, being hunted by furniture, Raven and Apple and Cerise and all our friends transformed. Forever after."

The red-haired wolf cub nuzzled Cedar's ankle.

"She's keeping the story going," Kitty said, nodding at me. Er, nodding at Maddie. "She's trying to take over for the Narrator."

"Well," Lizzie said, "today is indeed a day of absurdicy and idiotity. But it is only right that the post be taken over by someone from our noble homeland. Carry on, Maddie. I will allow it."

"Okay, first priority, we need to figure out what to do now," said Cedar. "What do you think, Lizzie? Should we try to find a way out of the school, or would that damage the magical barrier that's keeping the Jabberwock in? Should we just keep hiding inside the hutling till the faculty gets rid of the Jabberwock?"

At the mention of the Jabberwock, Kitty's face went big-eyed and wince-y.

"Kitty Cheshire," Lizzie said all loud and grand-like, "disappear your way out of the school, beyond the magic barrier, and find Headmaster Grimm."

Kitty's nose went wrinkle-winkly, and she opened her mouth as if she would hiss. But instead, she shrugged and disappeared as Lizzie had suggested. Or ordered. Or something.

Kitty reappeared again a minute later, her Cheshire grin still grinning but not in a happy-making way. Now she did hiss.

"I can't. I'm trapped by the barrier, too. I do *not* like being trapped."

"Maddie, what do you think?" asked Cedar.

But Maddie had a hard time thinking about the problem and the solving. Maddie was too busy fretting, and fretting was a thing Maddie was not very good at, having had very little practice.

HIGGLEDY-PIGGLEDY PUDDING OF RYE, KISS THE BOOK AND NEVER CRY.

"Oh!" Maddie said aloud. "I think the not-me-Narrator is trying to give us a clue."

Maddie repeated the higgledy-and-cry bit. Kitty and Lizzie both nodded as if she'd just said something very un-boring, but Cedar rubbed her new, real eyes and shook her new, real head, worried that these Wonderlandians were as touched by the muddling magic as Daring-beastie and Raven-raven.

Wait, how do I...that is, how did Maddie know what Cedar was thinking and feeling? Maddie never had before, not unless she overheard the Narrator gabbing about it.

KISS THE BOOK.

Maddie had a library book in her backpack. She pulled it out: *A Narrative History of the Grand Craft of Narration, by Narrators Anonymous.* She scanned the first chapter, "Narration Basics."

"We'll just sit here while you read a book, then," Lizzie said.

"According to the book," said Maddie, "Narrators have splendid, magicky insight into characters' thoughts and motivations. This insight usually only comes after years of training, but some Narrators have so much desire to storytell, their skills come more quickly. Tea-riffic! Ooh, and did you know that the Narration Board writes down all of Ever After's narrated stories? The Narration Board prints them and sends them to libraries and bookstores. Real people far, far away might actually read what I narrate here! So hexciting!"

"What people?" asked Cedar. "How?"

"I don't know, but our conversation is probably being written down right now. And in fact, in the slippy-slinky way of time, somewhere in the Lands and Otherlands, someone could be reading it at this very moment."

Maddie leaned forward, squinting, and for the barest second, the world of cottages and castles and forests and magic parted, and she spied, far, far away and yet as close as her nose, someone holding the story she was narrating. A reader.

(That's *you*.) Maddie winked. (Go ahead and wink back.)

Maddie caught her breath. The story she was helping to tell had the power to connect characters and readers. This narration thing was as delightful as a bag of goldyfish!

Seemingly by its own power, the narration book flipped to another page near the back.

"Oh, to become a real Narrator—even just a temporary one—I'm supposed to take the Narrator's Oath. Okey-dokey, here I go." Maddie read aloud the oath. "'I, your name here, hereby take—'"

"I don't think you actually say 'your name here,'" said Cedar. "You probably say your *actual* name."

"Oh! Well, that doesn't make much sense, but all right. 'I, Madeline Hatter, hereby take the sacred Oath of Narration. I swear to: only speak the truth; follow the story wherever it may lead; observe all that happens but report only the most important and interesting parts; honor the characters in both their greatness and their mistakes; serve only the story and the reader and no other, be it king or queen or baker or candlestick maker; and never, ever, ever, ever, ever interfere with the story. Ever.

"'If I so do my best, may this story be recorded and printed and zipped and zapped into hands and eyes and ears and minds and hearts everywhere, and may it no longer be my story but belong to each reader who drinks it in, to make them bigger or smaller as needed; to fill in those tiny holes and smooth over the rough places; to make them sigh and laugh and dream and wonder; to pass a lonely afternoon or enliven a dull evening; to in every regard do just what a story is supposed to do, which is become whatever each reader needs most at that moment. And for this noble mission I pledge my skills and shortcomings, my talents and my weaknesses, until The End.'"

Maddie exhaled. Everything was so quiet you could hear the cottage breathing.

"Did the oath work?" Cedar asked. "Are you officially our Narrator? Can the story go on?"

"I think so," said Maddie. "I feel less worried, but we won't know if it worked till the story is over."

And in the meantime, I'll keep narrating the story! Oh wait, a Narrator isn't supposed to say "I." That rule was in Chapter One. But in my experience, they do sometimes say *ahem*.

So, *ahem*. The girls sat in the walking cottage and argued about what to do next.

"It doesn't seem fair," said Cedar, as the Raven-raven alighted on her head. "Some got so changed they can't speak anymore while I got what I've always wanted."

"I suspect the Blue-Haired Fairy laid deep magic on you, Cedar," said Maddie. "Maybe you were preprogrammed to change into a real girl, and so when the Jabberwock magic touched you, instead of turning into a plank of cedarwood or something, it triggered your change magic. You became real."

"Maddie, you are really smart."

"Am I? I wonder if that's new, or if I've always been smart."

"You've always been smart, Maddie," Lizzie said idly as she peered out the window. She seemed to realize she'd spoken that aloud, cleared her throat, and proclaimed, "But I, too, am quite bright! Exceptionally so! More than most!"

"If the Jabberwock is turning Ever After into Wonderland, why aren't you guys excited?" asked Cedar.

"*That* isn't Wonderland." Kitty pointed out the

window, where giant pumpkins with wheels were ramming into each other. "*You* said it, Cedar. It's out of order. All messed up."

Outside the window, one of the pumpkins cracked apart with the impact, spilling seeds onto the ground, which were then gobbled up by a crazed legion of red paper envelopes.

"It's not Wonderlandish at all," Lizzie said. She paused, afraid to admit there was something wrong that she couldn't just rule into submission. But sad truth pressed up into her throat, and she let the words out. "Ever After cannot be transformed into Wonderland, not even by magic. The Jabberwock tries, but it comes out wrong, a hybrid of two places, being neither. A monster making monsters."

"Its magic is tearing things from the names they were and turning everything mad," said Maddie.

Cedar looked confuse-boggled, but Maddie's mind was Narrator-sharp, and so she tried to explain.

"Madness is life, but the *unpredictable* parts of life. See, a person is alive and so might do anything. A chair is not, so you know what it's going to do: just sit there." Maddie pointed to one of the school chairs outside, barking at the hutling. "Now that *that* chair is alive, it's no longer predictable. It might do anything, just like a person. The school and everything in it are turning mad. Nothing does what you expect. It's all unpredictable. It's all mad."

"But not the *right* sort of madness," said Kitty.

Lizzie pressed her fingers against the windowpane. "In Wonderland, a chair *knows* it is a chair. But things touched by the Jabberwock madness no longer know what they are. It's royally disappointing, like being promised hot tea and getting swamp juice in your teacup."

"Ooh, nice simile, Lizzie," said Maddie.

"The Jabberwock's magic is forcing things to be what they are not," said Cedar. "That *is* the wrong kind of madness." *And so is this whole Royal and Rebel dilemma*, Cedar thought.

The Raven-raven hopped onto Cedar's knee, and she petted the bird's wings, so black they glimmered with a sheen of purple. Headmaster Grimm's trying to force Raven to be evil was like the Jabberwock's forcing chairs to walk around and roar. Perhaps Royals were the people who would do the things they were supposed to do in their stories anyway. But Rebels wouldn't naturally do what their destinies tried to force them to do. And forced destinies could wreak as much havoc as a Jabberwock.

It was suddenly so clear to Cedar! She decided she should explain her insight to Headmaster Grimm. If she ever saw him again.

The chair herd had grown larger. They began clacking folding seats, stomping steel-tipped legs, and flinging one another at the hutling's door. The hutling *baaaaked* and *braaaaked* and darted about. The room swayed.

"This much madness is dangerous," said Cedar, sliding into a wall.

"I wonder if Alice felt like we do now when she fell down the rabbit hole," said Lizzie.

Kitty began quoting a well-known Wonderland poem:

Down she goes, like a blown nose
to expose what is under is not the ground
and once she arrives she finds that she's found.

Maddie said, "Since Wonderland is often found down, maybe things get madder the lower you go, and the school will become less mad the higher we climb."

"We'd still be trapped here by the magical barrier," said Cedar, "but at least it might be less dangerous."

"Up, hut-beast! I command you to take us up!" said Lizzie.

Cedar crouched by the fireplace and whispered into the chimney, "Hutling? We're hoping the top of the school might be safer than down here with clacking and stampeding chairs." She stroked its fuzzy wallpaper like the neck of a frisky horse. "Could you carry us up? Please?"

The cottage began to run. Cedar gripped the mantel, trying to stay on her soft, little feet as the cottage swayed and bounced. The floor tilted back as the hutling started up the stairs. Kitty slipped, rolling back and hitting the wall. She dissolved and reappeared beside Cedar.

"I'm bored," said Kitty. "This is taking forever."

She put her hands beneath the curtains and began to tickle. The hutling howled, the whole cottage rumbling.

"Stop bugging it," said Cedar.

Kitty disappeared and reappeared at the other window, her feet on the sill, pulling the curtains as if they were the reins on a galloping horse.

"Yee-ha," she said with her mischievous smile.

The hutling rumbled again. The walls squeezed in as if the cottage were tightening up its middle, and the girls all squished together. Kitty's face was pressed into Cedar's cheek, and Maddie's head was in Lizzie's armpit. The hutling opened its door and the back wall spasmed forward, effectively spitting the girls out. They landed on the stairs.

"Pick us back up!" Lizzie shouted.

The hutling shut its door and ran away, its chicken-feet toenails tapping on the stone steps.

"Wait! The Raven-raven!" said Cedar. "And the Apple-apple! And all the other people-things!"

"Bah. They're safer in there," said Lizzie.

Cedar folded her arms. "Kitty, why did you—"

"I am *not* reasonable," said Kitty, smiling but not meaning it. "I refuse to be turned reasonable by that horribific monster's magic. I am a Cheshire. I am chaos! But this kind of chaos, I don't...I don't know what to..." She turned red in the face and disappeared.

"Kitty Cheshire!" Lizzie shouted at the air. "I order you to be chaotic again!"

Smile first, Kitty reappeared. "Thanks, Lizzie," she whispered.

From the darkness down the corridor, Cedar heard slow clopping like the sound a twelve-burner stove would make if it could walk. Then a hideous, scratchy voice whispered, "I. Eat. Wiggly. Things."

Cedar screamed. She took the stairs three at a time, running higher and higher, the other girls following. Well, Kitty never ran, but when they reached the top of the stairs, Kitty appeared there, terror in her smiling eyes.

The scratchy whisper echoed up from the floor below. "Wiggly? Things?"

And Cedar kept running. Her new legs ached, her thighs trembling, but she didn't stop climbing stairs until suddenly she was going down.

"Eek! How did that happen?" Cedar reversed to go back up, passing the other girls. "Come on, we've got to go *up*."

"We are going up," Kitty said with a laugh.

"Close your eyes at once," said Lizzie. "You are being tricked by reality."

Cedar closed her eyes. Maddie took her hand. And they started running back up the stairs. When Cedar peeked, they appeared to be going down, so she shut her eyes again and *felt* rather than *saw* the climb.

They only stopped when they reached the highest tower of the school. It was wobbling as if made of rubber.

Cedar clutched the empty frame of the window, its panes curiously missing. Outside, the huge yellow dome of the magical barrier crackled and fizzed as insects flew into it. Through the yellow-ness she spotted the Troll Bridge and, beyond, the rooftops of Book End.

Maddie rummaged through her Hat of Many Things. So helpful, really, wearing a Hat of Many Things. She wondered why everyone didn't have one. Then she scolded herself for wondering about something that didn't matter to the current story. That's simply not what Narrators do! Hocus focus, Maddie. *Ahem.*

From her hat, she pulled out two telescopes, holding one to each eye.

"There's Dad!" said Maddie. "He's on the roof of

the Tea Shoppe. He sees me. Dad! Dad!" Maddie shouted, waving. "Oh, good. He's got the flags."

"Flags?" asked Cedar.

"Yes, to spell out messages from far away. Doesn't everyone have a flag language with their father?" asked Maddie. "Okay, he's signaling with the flags. I'll translate. 'If the Jabberwock magic reaches Book End, everything ends. Because our story will literally become the book end and the book will end without a resolution.' Oh nose!"

Lizzie grabbed one of the telescopes and put it to her eye. "No way he said all that so fast. Wait...oh!...You're right, Maddie." She handed the telescope back to Maddie. "Your dad can really move flags."

"Our story ends? That can't be right," Cedar started to say, but then, really, what *was* right at the moment? She'd just spotted the glass panes that were missing from the windows. They were slowly crawling across the tower wall, rippling like transparent caterpillars.

"Cedar, could you stop noticing things for a minute?" Maddie said. "You're the main character of this chapter, so I'm supposed to focus more on you, but I can't narrate what you're doing and pay attention to my dad at the same time."

"Sorry."

"Thanks. Okay, he says the Jabberwock can't complete the transformation of Ever After into its version of Wonderland without Wonderland things to squeeze. Things of Wonderland are full of Wonder, and Wonder powers its magic. At least I think that's what he's saying. He's speaking Riddlish. With flags."

"So, wait..." Cedar said. "The Jabberwock needs to collect Wonderland things and use them like batteries for its magic? Wonderland things like... like you guys?"

Kitty and Lizzie backed away from the window, and the tippy tower slid them farther. They bumped together, Kitty's pale purple locks tangled in Lizzie's gold crown.

"Off... with her head," Lizzie said, but she sounded more like she was saying, *I'm so scared at the moment I may start beheading butter people.*

Kitty snickered.

"What?" Lizzie demanded.

"Nothing," said Kitty. "Narration joke."

"Dad is warning us to stay away from the Jabber-wock," Maddie said. "If it captures the three of us, it would have enough power to make its mad transformation permanent."

"Yeah, I'd planned to avoid it," said Cedar. "But where is it?"

Kitty, her smile gone stiff, whispered through her teeth, "*Right. There.*"

Cedar whirled around. Through another window, she could see the Jabberwock hanging on the side of a tower, gripping the stones with long white claws. It was as large as a full-size dragon armored with gray scales, but its feet and antennaed head were ragged with unexpected fur. Its snakelike neck and toothy head were stretched forward, its milky white, seemingly blind eyes staring at something in the distance. Toward Book End.

It screeched and beat its huge leathery wings, lifting off the tower and taking flight.

"It sees Dad!" said Maddie. "It will squeeze him for Wonder and then he'll be Wonder-less and we've got to stop it!"

"Baba Yaga's magic barrier will stop it," Cedar whispered.

The Jabberwock threw itself at the transparent yellow dome, with an explosion of flares and sparks. The beast shrieked but seemed more angry than hurt. It attacked the barrier again and again and again. The yellow of the magic began to dim, like egg yolks bleeding into the whites. The barrier was weakening. And the Mad Hatter was on the other side. Maddie's Dad. No, not Dad!

"No!" Maddie found herself screaming. "Leave him alone!"

The long, thin neck snaked around, the gruesome face of the Jabberwock pointed at their tower.

It shrieked, beating its wings straight for them.

Run, said the Narrator.

"Run," Maddie said.

They ran.

They were only halfway down the first flight of stairs when the tower shook with the impact of the Jabberwock.

The stone steps underneath Cedar's feet suddenly felt softer, almost gelatinous. She slipped but kept running on the stairs in the same direction, though sometimes she felt that she was going up, not down. She heard the Jabberwock shriek, and the tower trembled and hummed and seemed a breath away from crumbling.

Cedar's new heart was pounding hard against her ribs, like a bird flinging itself against a window, trying to escape. She began to cry but couldn't marvel at the newness and wonder of cold wetness sliding down her soft cheeks. Instead, tears felt like losing control, like the ground no longer under her shoes, like hurting and not being sure if she'd ever feel okay again. She stumbled into the soft floor and began to slowly sink. Maddie grabbed her hands and started to pull, but Cedar wondered if it was too late.

She whispered the truth aloud: "Maybe everything is easier when you're made of wood."

No, she told herself. *No!* She'd been waiting her entire life to be real. She was not going to let the fear of a Jabberwock steal that away.

"That's right," said Maddie. "You are not made of wood, you are made of Wood. You are Cedar Wood!"

I am Cedar Wood. Cedar pulled herself out of the sinking floor and ran faster. No more waiting. Now she was who she'd always wanted to be. And whatever happened next, she'd make this chance count.

CHAPTER 16

RUNNING FROM DEADLY TERROR

THE GIRLS RAN. THE WALLS GROANED WITH stress, and each painting they passed only compounded their worry.

"It's right behind you!" yelled a girl in a painting holding a watering can.

"It will eat us all!" shouted a painting of a wide-mouthed man on a bridge.

"Run, stinky pooters, run," the daisies in a bright watercolor chanted.

"Behave!" Lizzie shouted at the daisies. "I am a

princess of Wonderland and I will not be insulted by stained canvas!"

The Narrator warned her to keep running, but Lizzie was all red-face and up-chin and pointing-finger, and didn't listen. The Jabberwock was right outside the window, looking in with those milk-white eyes that seemed blind and yet saw. It opened its square, toothy mouth.

"Duck!" Cedar shouted.

"Where?" said Lizzie, looking around for a duck.

Cedar pulled her down just as the Jabberwock hissed, a spray of magic exhaling over their heads. The paint on the walls curdled and flaked off, pulling itself together into a huge mass of daddy longlegs. The paint-spiders began to crawl all over the girls, tickling them with their feather-light feet.

Cedar screamed. "Stop it! I'm finally real, and I'm not going to waste this realness getting attacked by tickle-spiders!"

Lizzie leaped into the path of the oncoming spiders, pointed her scepter, and commanded, "Retreat, multilegged paint chips! Do not touch my friend!"

Cedar blinked. So did Maddie. Lizzie swallowed. Had she just admitted to having friends? Her mother would not approve. All this madness was making it hard to keep her mother's good advice in mind.

The girls shook off the spiders and kept running. SNAILS DON'T ROCK OR ROLL.

Behave now, not-me-Narrator! You know better than to interrupt a story.

"Where do we go?" Cedar asked.

"If it doesn't matter where you end up, any path will do," said Kitty.

"But I do know where I want to end up," said Cedar. "Away!"

"There is no getting to Away," said Kitty. "Away is wherever we aren't."

"Then let's make sure the Jabberwock stays in Away," said Lizzie.

Ahead, several tiny cows with pink butterfly wings hovered in the corridor, gripping wands between their bitty hooves.

"Are those the fairy-godmothers-in-training?" Cedar said. "The FiGITs?"

"DiGITs," Kitty whispered.

Above the crowd of cows fluttered tiny cheese slices and milk cartons on wispy wings.

"Right. *Dairy*-godmothers-in-training," Lizzie said.

"Help us?" said Cedar.

One winged cow pointed her magic wand at Cedar. Cedar ducked just as a pink bolt of magic flew over her head. The vase in the nook behind her turned into a large glass pitcher full of milk.

"Keep running!" Lizzie said.

Shrinking down to the size of a dog, the Jabberwock darted through an open window. It flapped behind them, its breath sizzling the air. The milk pitcher melted and covered the floor, making it slick as ice. The girls slipped and slid and almost fell.

They turned a corner, and all fell flat to the floor as fire shot through the air, temporarily slowing the miniature Jabberwock. Squinting to see the source of the fire, Maddie spotted a four-wheeled cart blocking the hall.

"A fire-breathing wagon," Kitty murmured. "Everything is Ever After and Wonderland confused together."

Lizzie smashed a window with her scepter. "Out," she said. "Everyone."

She helped Maddie up to the sill and waited for Cedar and Kitty to escape before she followed. Her expression was slightly puzzled, as if she wasn't sure why she wasn't going first.

The girls grabbed hold of the ivy growing over the outside of the school and climbed down. The vines giggled. The vines sighed. Giggles and sighs come from mouths. And things with mouths can bite.

"Don't bite," Lizzie ordered the vines. "At least, don't bite us."

STARS IN YOUR EYES! FOAM IN YOUR BEARD!

Not now, not-me-Narrator. I'm trying to work here.

So the girls were hanging from the vines when the Jabberwock appeared above them, again as huge as a dragon, which is even huger than a wagon. Its three-toed feet reached, claws clinking, sharp as the edges of things.

Cedar screamed. Maddie would have screamed,

too, but she was too busy concentrating on the narration.

And then the vines opened their leafy mouths and began to bite the Jabberwock. It clawed at the ivy, giving the girls a second to drop down onto another windowsill and climb into a new room. It was—

BEES KNEES DON'T BEND UNLESS WELL-HONEYED.

Stop interrupting, not-me-Narrator. Don't you see how hard it is to narrate a story? All this running from deadly terror is happening too fast! I'm getting thinking pains as it is, trying to imitate your talkage and wordage and not get too wonderlandiful in my descriptions 'cause that's not how *you* would do it. When you were normal, anyway. And—*ack!*

A crab slightly smaller than Maddie grabbed her hands in its claws and began to dance. Each girl was claimed by a similar partner. An overlarge oyster at the front of the room counted time. "One, two, one, two, heel, toe, slide…" And meanwhile, outside the window, the Jabberwock was clawing its way free from the vines.

Lizzie fought out of her partner's grip and swung open the room's only door.

"Keep dancing!" shouted the oyster. "There are no makeup days for crab-dancing class!"

The girls followed Lizzie out the door, shutting it behind—

DON'T TRUST YOUR LEFT LEG.

Please, not-me-Narrator, this is getting out of control. I need you to behave yourself so I can concentrate, okay? Please? Pretty please with shoelaces on top?

MUFF.

Is that a yes? You'll behave now and let me narrate?

MUFF.

I'll take that as a yes. *Ahem.* And so they kept running, the Jabberwock always close behind, each new hall and room more dangerous than the last. Just when they thought they'd found a safe place—

SCOODLE-MOO EAT A DOO.

Argh!

CHAPTER 17

TALES OF WANDERING UN-BOOKS

LIZZIE HAD *HAD* IT WITH RUNNING. IT WAS bad enough when Coach Gingerbreadman made them run, run as fast as they could in Grimmnastics class, but running just to stay alive was unseemly. They had turned a corner and had finally lost sight of that despicable Jabberwock when the walls shook with the sound of a battering ram. Lizzie stumbled.

"Off with its head!" she yelled automatically.

"Wait, when the rest of the building shook, that red door didn't move," said Cedar.

The red heart-shaped door looked exactly like the one in Lizzie's dorm that transported her into the Grove. This galloping corridor definitely wasn't her dorm, but nothing looked like itself anymore. Perhaps the door had traveled, searched her out, even. A certain tingle tickled Lizzie's hand when she turned the doorknob.

The Jabberwock rounded the corner behind them. Magic hissed from its huge mouth, melting reality.

"In!" Lizzie yelled. She pushed Cedar, Kitty, and Maddie through first and then jumped after them, slamming it shut. She leaned against it, expecting the pounding of the Jabberwock trying to force its way through the door, but it never came.

The air had changed, warm, soft, quiet. They were no longer in the school. They were in the Grove. Lizzie's center relaxed just a little, and strangely she thought she might cry. Which was absurd. Crying was not relaxing at all. Right?

"You saved us," Cedar said.

"I *pushed* you," Lizzie said.

"You pushed us into safety," Cedar said.

"Through the door that you noticed," Lizzie said. "So, technically, *you* saved us."

Cedar reached out to take Lizzie's hand. "Thanks, Lizzie."

Cedar's thank-you made Lizzie feel all huggable and candy-sweet, and she had to fight the ridiculous urge to say a thank-you back.

"Thank…uh, I'll thank you to take back that gratitude as soon as you are able," Lizzie grumbled. "It is unseemly."

The Grove looked exactly as Lizzie had left it, unchanged, un-Jabberwocked. The beast's magic was running rampant in the school castle but, trapped by the barrier, it had not reached beyond into the school grounds. So far the Grove and, thankfully, Book End were safe. Lizzie breathed in again, relishing the familiar scents of spicy flowers, sweet tree sap, and minty grass. This was the smell of Wonderland. Of *real* Wonderland. Like her, it was between Wonderland and Ever After. The thought gave Lizzie strength.

"Not that I'm complaining," Kitty said, "but why didn't the Jabberwock just tear down that door and eat us?"

"This is a special place," Lizzie said, confident it was true.

"Hey, if that door transported us outside the school, then we're beyond the magic barrier, right?" said Cedar. "We can go find the faculty!"

Cedar began to run.

"Stop!" Lizzie yelled. Feeling so huggable-sweet and thanky had been uncomfortable. Time to shout orders again.

Hedgehogs nosed around in the grass near Lizzie's feet. She grabbed one and threw it, hitting Cedar's shoulder.

"Ow!" Cedar yelled. The hedgehog dropped to the ground and scampered away. "Poor little thing! Don't hurt it!"

It was not hurt at all, the Narrator was twiddly anxious to assure the reader. Wonderlandian hedge-hogs are bred for sports and in fact frequently nap their way through a croquet game in which they are the balls.

Lizzie picked up another hedgehog.

"Stop throwing animals at me," said Cedar.

"I'm not. You just got in the way," Lizzie said, flinging the creature over Cedar's shoulder. The hedgehog stopped suddenly as if it had struck an invisible wall. The air buzzed with the impact and brightened to a deep yellow. The hedgehog dropped to the ground, twitched, and wobbled back to the grass.

"Oh! We're still inside the magic barrier," Cedar said.

When Ever After High was normal, the heart-shaped door had sent Lizzie from her dorm to the Grove, which was on the edge of the school grounds. But it seemed even the door couldn't transport them outside Baba Yaga's barrier. If they were in the Grove yet still inside the magic barrier, then the barrier had made an extra bubble around the Grove to trap whatever tried to escape the school.

"Are we safe?" Cedar asked. "Can we just wait here till the teachers figure out how to fix everything?"

"Or until the monster figures out how to get in?" Kitty echoed.

"Hey, I have a signal!" Cedar said, punching numbers on her MirrorPhone. "We must be far enough away from the—Hello? Headmaster Grimm? This is Cedar Wood."

His irritated voice crackled on the speaker for all to hear. *"Miss Wood, do not bother me right now. We are very busy—watch out for that pixie!—very busy* concocting a spell to banish the Jabber—we need three more cockroaches!—banish the Jabberwock."

"Ugh! They don't know what they're doing!" Lizzie shouted. "Tell them an Ever Afterish spell won't work!"

"It won't?" Cedar asked in a small voice.

"Not the right kind of magic," Kitty said. "I can't believe they don't know the only thing that can defeat the Jabberwock."

Maddie nodded solemnly. Lizzie recited part of the poem aloud.

> He took his vorpal sword in hand:
> Long time the manxome foe he sought—
> So rested he by the Tumtum tree ...

"The vorpal sword, Headmaster!" Cedar said into her MirrorPhone. "You need the vorpal sword, like that poem says! Only the vorpal sword can defeat—"

"*The vorpal sword is in Wonderland, Miss' Wood,*" said the headmaster. "*And all portals into Wonderland are sealed. So we will use—newt eyeballs! Rumpel-stiltskin, we need more newt eyeballs!—will use a spell. Get to safety and kindly don't interrupt me again.*"

Click.

Cedar stared at the phone for some time. Kitty faded into a soft shadow. Maddie sat on the grass.

"So...so we have no hope?" said Cedar. "Raven will be a raven forever? Daring a beastie-thing? Hunter a tree? And we'll live out the rest of our lives inside this Grove?"

Maddie took Cedar's hand. Kitty reappeared, sitting with her back to them, but after a moment, she curled up on the grass, her head on Maddie's lap.

"Their spell might do *some*thing," Kitty said. "I guess."

Lizzie was tired. The more time she spent with these girls, the more she was reminded that she felt things. Helpy things. Unselfy things. Crawling feelings like worry and hope. Burn-ish feelings like fondness and friendliness. And worst of all, sappy grabby feelings like Concern For Others.

Lizzie opened her mother's deck of cards and found the one she was searching for:

♥

Above all else, avoid these things: vats of poison, Jabberwocks, paper cuts on fingertips, and Concern For Others.

If ever you detect Concern For Others
squirming into you,
shout at people till the feeling goes away.
Or the people do.

♥

"Off with your heads!" Lizzie shouted. "Off with all your heads! I am a princess of Wonderland and I…I…I am shouting at you!"

"Um…" said Cedar.

Lizzie's blood was up now. Enough feeling things Mother had forbidden her to feel. And enough waiting. A queen, even a queen-in-waiting, does not wait. Especially if you're a mad queen. And Lizzie *was* mad.

"I am going to fix this ridiculousness, as it appears no one else will, so things can return to as they were and I don't have to crawl with worry and feel burn-ish and battle Concern For Others!" Lizzie shouted.

The Narrator could tell that Lizzie was not really angry, just anxious, but did not make the observation aloud. Just as she didn't observe how the meticulous tending of the Grove revealed just how desperately Lizzie missed Wonderland.

"Wonderland!" said Maddie. "Someone of Wonderland would understand better than Headmaster Grimm."

Kitty admitted, "I've been trying to phone the White Queen without luck."

"Same with my dad," said Maddie. "But there is someone in Wonderland I sometimes talk to."

"What? Who?" Lizzie still felt choked by that unfortunate hope-ish thing perched in her chest. "Tell me at once! How dare you keep a someone of Wonderland a secret from your future queen!"

"There's a book I sometimes find that has a letter in it," Maddie said. "When I write back, the letter-writer responds, and I just know the writer is in Wonderland because he or she writes such Wonderlandish things. The book was in the library once. At other times inside a stocking, on top of a chimney, at the bottom of a bucket of frogs, beneath a bag of marshmallows..."

"Tales of wandering un-books is exactly what we shouldn't be wasting time on," Lizzie said, pacing. She had to solve this by herself, but she couldn't think when everyone was nattering on so.

"What does the letter writer write?" Cedar asked.

Lizzie realized they weren't going to hush up, so she stalked off to gather a few hedgehogs. Hedgehogs always got people's attention.

"The first letter just said, 'My ears itch,'" said Maddie. "Another said, 'Clap your hands if you can read this.'"

One hedgehog, two...Lizzie would need at least three, one for each of them. Maybe some extras in case she missed.

"I wrote a letter about all the things in Wonderland I missed," said Maddie, "and the letter writer told me how things are now. It made me feel less homesick."

Lizzie grabbed one of the hedgehog balls and cocked her arm back but was stopped by a thought. It was not an *Off with your head!* kind of thought. Nevertheless, inside Lizzie's head, beneath her red-streaked black hair and impressive gold crown, it felt big and important and as wonderful as Wonderland.

"Maddie?" Lizzie dropped the hedgehogs, and they scampered away. "Do you think this mysterious

Wonderlandian might know how we could get the vorpal sword?"

"Ooh, that is a big and important and wonderlandiful thought, Lizzie!" Maddie reached into her hat and pulled out a small leather-bound book with the title *Hutch and Housing for Hare and Architect*.

"Ah-ha! Here it is!" said Maddie. "What luck! It's never been in my hat before."

Maddie flipped through the pages and came to a small red envelope. Lizzie grabbed it and tore it open. The letter was handwritten and stamped with a bunny paw print at the bottom.

"'Life in a poisoned land is actually less poisonous than it is lonely,'" Lizzie read. Her voice tripped over the word *lonel*y, the word going as wobbly as her middle. She touched the bunny paw print. "Very well, then. Let's put this leather-bound postman to the test. Someone, fetch paper and pen!"

Maddie rummaged in her hat and managed to find scraps of notepaper and a pen.

"Cedar, you will scribe for me, as you do the Artsing and the Craftsing," said Lizzie.

Then she dictated in her most queenly voice:

Book Letter Person/Animal/Thing—
Your princess requests knowledge.
Knowledge of the type and ilk and substance
of which one would seek when longing to rid
oneself of a pesky pest. Namely, a Jabberwock.
We need the vorpal sword in Ever After.
But how? And wherewith? And ho-hum?
Respond immediately.
Lizzie Hearts, Your Princess of Hearts, etc.

"Um," Cedar said, a little nervously. "Have you ever written a letter before, Lizzie?"

"Of course I have," Lizzie said, fairly certain that wasn't true. "Why? What's wrong with it?"

Cedar held her breath as if afraid to let the truth out.

"Why are you holding your breath?" Lizzie asked.

"Oh. It's so new. The breathing. I sometimes forget to do it," Cedar lied. And then widened her eyes.

"Cedar?" Maddie asked. "Did you just…?"

"I just forgot to breathe," Cedar lied again, smiling. "Also, I really like eating…um…porridge with mustard!"

Cedar folded up the letter and stuffed it in the book.

"Plus," Cedar said, "I once buried myself in the dirt up to my neck to see if I would grow."

"That *is* odd," Lizzie said, "though I suppose a reasonable scientific experiment."

"And I *did* grow," Cedar continued, laughing with delight. "Into a giant walking tree! And I...I lived for a hundred years in the Otherlands, battling giants and baking award-winning cupcakes."

"That explains a lot," Lizzie said, not really paying attention. "Where is the book?"

"Right over here," Cedar said, pointing at a spot on the grass that was just grass. "Whoa. It really was right here a second ago. I swear I'm not lying. Now."

Maddie nodded. "It does that," she said.

"Where is it?" Lizzie sputtered. "We need it!"

"We have to *find* it," said Maddie. "It's one of those kind of books."

CHAPTER 18

20% MORE VORPAL

CEDAR WOOD LIED. CEDAR WOOD LIED!

The girls were scrambling around the Grove, searching for the book, but Cedar could only wander, her mind spinning and tumbling about with the thought: *I lied!*

Apparently, when the Jabberwock's magic triggered her deep-rooted transformation into a real girl, it also undid that thorny honesty curse. She was free! She didn't have to blurt and blab. She could choose her own words—she could choose her own life!

Cedar knelt down, relishing the press of the grass against her knees, the tickle of a dangling flower on her ankle. She leaned over to look for the book under a bush of white roses dripping red paint, when a thought caught inside her like a fish on a sharp hook.

If her honesty curse was undone, was her "caring" and "kindness" curse undone, too?

Cedar straightened up and let her feelings probe her fast-beating heart. No more lies. Now she would have to discover the truth. Who was she really, beneath the wooden body and cursed-to-care-ness? Without the Blue-Haired Fairy's magic, was she still the girl who would do anything for her friends? Or, when faced with danger, would she and her tender body run away?

Cedar looked up and found Maddie looking back. Maddie, as the Narrator, knew Cedar's thoughts. She smiled encouragingly. Cedar nodded, but her heart still beat in rapid, shallow gasps. *No more lies, not even to myself. So who am I?*

They scoured the Grove three times over. Cedar checked her pockets, even though they weren't big enough to hold a book. Yet another truth fell on her, heavy as a stone—they might have to go back into that Jabberwock-infested school to find the book. The search could take forever! Lost things were always in the last place you looked.

"That's so true, Cedar!" Maddie said aloud. "You always find things the last place you look, so let's skip the middle part and just look in the last place."

"You make perfect sense, Hatworm," said Lizzie.

"Okay, let's all decide we're done looking after the next place," said Maddie.

Lizzie shut her eyes. "I am done."

"So done," said Kitty.

"Done!" said Cedar, meaning it. Wonderland logic could be fun.

Maddie got a serious look on her face. Well, she couldn't see her own face, but it felt impressively serious. She put out her hands and let them lead her to the Last Place. She crouched down by Cedar, unlaced Cedar's left boot, pulled it off, and removed the book.

"Whoa!" Cedar said. "I'm feeling *everything* today. You'd think I could feel a book in my boot."

She opened the letter and read:

Princess—

    We were overjoyed to receive your letter! You are beamishly correct, of course. The only way to defeat the Jabberwock is with the vorpal sword, which is thrust in the left-most bole of the fourth wabe of Tumtum trees. Alas, I cannot send it to you with words. I consulted with an owl, who informed me that with just the right picture, meticulously painted in fluxberry shades, you might be able to pluck it out of Wonderland, though such has never been done. Good luck!

Lizzie threw a handy hedgehog at Cedar. "Paint," she said.

"The letter said the sword is in Wonderland...." Cedar said.

"So what are you waiting for?" Lizzie made shooing motions with her hands. "Go do art!"

The Narrator had some distance from the action and was able to see how, sometimes, Lizzie just didn't explain things very clearly. Especially to people outside her own head.

"Cedar, we can't get to Wonderland," said Maddie. "But maybe if you paint the sword here in this Wonderlandish Grove, the magic of Wonderland could make it real and within our reach."

"Really? But I can't," Cedar said. She pulled a leather pouch out of her skirt pocket. "I have my brushes but they're useless without paints, and I don't even know what it is supposed to look like!"

"It's a sword," Lizzie said. She pulled a butter knife out of her own pocket. "Like this, but bigger." She held it up and closed one eye. "Also with more vorpal. Like, twenty percent more vorpal."

"But…" Cedar looked at her hands. Her real, fleshy, soft hands. She'd never drawn anything with a real hand before. Doubt pumped through her like blood. "Well, to begin with, I'm going to need a better description than just 'sword.'"

"A *vorpal* sword," Lizzie said.

"It seems to me," Kitty cut in, "that descriptions of things, especially the good ones that actually make you brain-picture something, come from Narrators."

"Good idea," Lizzie said. "Maddie, narrate a detailed description of the vorpal sword for Cedar."

Good descriptions come from good Narrators. Okay, then.

"There's a tree in Wonderland," said Maddie. "A Tumtum tree. And it looks as trees do. You know, with the trunk and the branches and the leaves that are sometimes green. And leaves are always moving about, so they're the unpredictable lifey part of an otherwise predictable tree."

"Come on, Maddie, you can do it," said Cedar. "Keep going. That was…good-ish."

"I'm new at this, and my brain is getting tired and isn't as springy and bouncy as it was. Plus, it's been so long since I saw a Tumtum tree. Or anything in Wonderland."

"Ooh, I bet other Narrators have described the vorpal sword and Tumtum trees," said Cedar. "We should just go look for a book in the library!"

She smiled. Then she frowned. Lizzie was already frowning. Kitty disappeared and then reappeared dangling upside down from a tree so that her constant smile seemed to turn into a frown. At first, Maddie thought they must be playing a frowning game and— what fun! Even a frowning game was still a game!

But then Maddie realized that they were frowning

because they had to get a book from the library. And the library was in the school. And the school was mad and haunted by the Jabberwock.

Now was a moment to find out who Cedar was without the curses. She took slow, deep breaths until she felt able to say what she absotively, never-aftery wanted to say.

"I'll do it," said Cedar. "I'll go out there to get the book. It's better that you Wonderlandians stay safe in here. If the Jabberwock captures me, it can't use me to power the permanent transformation of Ever After."

"Cedar, your knees are knocking together," said Lizzie.

"No, they're not," said Cedar.

But they were. She hadn't realized, because in the past when her wooden knees knocked together, they made a tapping sound.

"I'll do it," she said again. "It doesn't matter if I am afraid. You're my friends, so I should do it."

Lizzie was watching Cedar very carefully. "You are brave, ex-puppet, to offer to do what scares you. But you must stay here, make paints, and prepare. I will retrieve the written word!"

Cedar exhaled again and didn't argue. But her real stomach flopped about, and she knew in a way that it wasn't her imagination but what people with guts called "a gut feeling," that this wouldn't be the last time she'd have to make that choice. To risk her new life for her friends. Or to save her new, real life and run away.

"Hold your sea horses!" said Maddie. "If Lizzie goes, I should go with her because it will be dangerous, and that's interesting, and Narrators are supposed to storytell the most interesting bits. But stuff will keep happening here with Cedar and Kitty that I wouldn't be able to narrate. Good gravy boats, but this is getting more complicated than a tea party underwater!"

"I can go by myself, thank you," said Lizzie.

"Not a fairy chance," said Maddie. "I took a sacred oath to tell this story. And this story has two main characters: Lizzie and Cedar. A real Narrator would know what Cedar was doing when Lizzie was away, but I'm not a real Narrator and I don't have all those powers."

"We'll tell you what happened here when you get back," said Cedar.

"But that'll be boring," said Maddie. "Everybody knows you can't just tell what happens. You have to *show* it."

"I don't think everybody knows that," Lizzie muttered.

"'Show Don't Tell' is an entire chapter in the narration book! I can't narrate Cedar's action *and* go with Lizzie!" said Maddie.

"I'll do it." Kitty was lying on her stomach in the grass, examining her nails.

"Do what?" asked Cedar.

"Narrate this part of Cedar's story. What's the matter with me, volunteering to do helpish things and *being involved*?" Kitty shuddered. "But since I've always been able to hear the Narrator, same as Maddie, I must share the ability to step in as an emergency Narrator. So I will be the emergency Narrator to the emergency Narrator."

Maddie crouched down and gave Kitty a kiss on her cheek.

"Uck!" Kitty licked the back of her hand and then wiped it on her cheek to clean off the kiss.

"Try to be talkative, Cedar," said Maddie. "That will make Kitty's job easier."

"Good luck, you two!" said Cedar. "Or as they say, break a leg!"

Lizzie straightened up taller and adjusted her crown. "Yes, we will break *all* the legs."

The heart-shaped door was waiting, hanging in midair with no wall to support it. Lizzie opened the door, revealing blackness beyond. She stood even straighter and stepped in first. Maddie took Earl Grey out of her hat, set him on the grass, and hopped after Lizzie. The door shut.

....

....

....

"Um, Kitty? Are you narrating? Kitty? You're not narrating, are you, Kitty?"

"Kitty shrugged."

"Kitty, I don't think you actually need to say what you're doing. Not out loud, anyway. Maddie said she narrated by *thinking* out loud."

I would like to pluck all the petals off those roses.

"Kitty, you didn't take the oath! I hope this works without taking the Narrator's Oath. Just remember to think aloud about what's happening so it gets written down somewhere."

My fingernails look amazing. Maddie's dormouse smells like waffles. Also, waffles are gross. I don't know what Gus and Helga were going on about.

"Try not to just think about what you would normally think about, Kitty. Don't use the word *I*. Observe what's happening and think your observations in nice, clean sentences. And make sure after I speak, you aloud-think 'Cedar said.'"

Cedar said.

Kitty Cheshire, the girl formally known as "I," observed things. She observed that Cedar Wood used to look like a scratching post. But now she was fleshy and soft. And now she was picking flux-berries in every shade from black to green to orange to pink and smooshing them onto big, broad leaves to use as paint. She also seemed more confident than normal, which somehow made Kitty Cheshire feel proud of her.

Kitty Cheshire was really bad at narrating. And the fact that she noticed a flaw in herself worried her. Clearly, Kitty Cheshire was no longer her perfect, indifferent self. Kitty Cheshire had been changed by the Jabberwock's magic. Kitty Cheshire was actually starting to care about other people's Happily Ever Afters.

The change magic was definitely getting stronger.

CHAPTER 19

YELLOW WALLPAPER

hugs?

LIZZIE MARCHED THROUGH HER SPECIAL heart-shaped door with what she hoped was absolutely no fear. But she feared there was fear. The hallway that had been on the other side of the door when they went in was gone. Instead, they entered a dark and cramped space, the only light trickling down from a dim circle at least thirty feet above their heads. The walls were old stone and slick with mossy slime. It felt for all the world like they were at the bottom of a well.

Lizzie reached behind her to feel the coarse wood of the heart-shaped door. She could go back. Cedar had said she would do it, and queens commanded other people—

"There are stairs," Maddie whispered, pointing.

Shoved into the wall of the "well" were short wooden struts just wide enough for a foot. If they were *very* careful, they might be able to make it to the top without falling to a painful death.

All the wild confidence she'd felt in her Wonderlandian Grove fizzled out of Lizzie. All marchiness chilled out of her feet.

But she whispered, "Off with its head."

Maddie nodded.

Lizzie shakily ascended the stairs. They were wet and soft, like slushy snow, so she had to lean against the slime-coated wall for support. Even the *shush, shush, shush* of their feet seemed too loud. The Jabberwock could be anywhere.

At last, Lizzie climbed out of the well and into the light of a carpeted space that was refreshingly hallway-shaped. It almost seemed like the normal school, but as they crept along, wrongness was everywhere. Slides instead of steps, curves instead of corners, the floor making soft *ribbit*s with every press of her feet. So much had transformed that Lizzie stared at an innocent lamp, waiting for it to sprout legs and dance a jig.

Fear neither lamps nor jigs, Lizzie, she told herself. *Just find the library.*

Lizzie had spent hours in the library, reading the Wonderlandian books, gazing at the illustrations. In the quiet grandeur of the library, she had let herself yearn for home, the way cheese yearns for cloth, the way bees yearn for bumble. So she knew the exact location of every Wonderland-related book: which corner, which wall, which shelf, and even which hidden chests in the back of custodial closets.

"That's good," Maddie whispered.

"*Hmph*." Lizzie did not approve of Maddie's nosing around her royal and private thoughts, but at the moment she was occupied with the larger worry of actually finding the library in a Jabberwocked school.

"That's bad," whispered Maddie.

Lizzie parted some drapes, trying to let in more light, only to find that the drapes covered blank stone walls and were themselves dripping with butter and grape jelly.

Everything Lizzie saw was twisted, neither Ever After nor Wonderland. Brushrooms grew out of the floor, wiggling their bristles at them. Treacle tapestries dripped on the wall, their shiny-sweet images ever-changing. A pot of flowers seemed to smile at her. That was delightfully Wonderlandish! Except that the smile was a little too intense. And when they opened their mouths, instead of singing, they lectured on mathematics.

Lizzie took her safety scissors out of her pocket to cut off their heads but thought better of it. What if those flowers had been Dexter or Darling or someone?

The hallway seemed to go on forever, far and away into the distance, until it flickered and abruptly ended.

Lizzie and Maddie shrank back as large chunks of the walls fell away and resolved themselves into further hallways. A gigantic caterpillar, each segment of its body a fringed throw pillow with tassel legs, stampeded across their path from the right hall to the left.

"That's odd," Maddie said.

"No doubt," Lizzie said. "At the very least, things should be moving left to right. It's as if the very rules of civil behavior are being ignored."

A gang of cards chased after the caterpillar, paper flapping obscenely as they ran. These were not respectable cards, to Lizzie's mind—that is, they were not *playing* cards. These were *greeting* cards, if what each of them was shouting was any clue.

"*Get well soon!*" yelled the first to cross their path.

"*Happy birthday,*" cheered the second. The third wetly spluttered, "*I'm so sorry.*"

The last card in the group noticed them, stopped, and pointed its long, thin arm threateningly.

"*Happy anniversary?*" it asked.

"Happy anniversary," Maddie said.

The card nodded its front flap and ran to catch up with its pack.

"That was close," said Lizzie. "I was about to say 'Condolences' and may have gotten us smooshed inside the card like pressed wildflowers."

They arrived in an open room that might have

once been the Castleteria. All the tables, chairs, and benches were huddled against one wall, shivering. The space left by their absence was empty, except for several upside-down bowls on the floor and a huge, lumpy gray ball in the center of the room under the chandelier. The gray ball sounded like it was giggling.

"Maybe we should go a different way," Maddie whispered. "This seems way too creepy to be safe."

"Laughing things are never dangerous," Lizzie said, marching forward.

The ball stopped laughing.

"You," Lizzie announced. "Giggling Thing! We need directions!"

The lumpy ball spun around, exposing raisin eyes and a wide-open mouth. Whatever it was, it looked *needy*. It plopped forward, its huge belly slapping the floor, its flat, walrus-like tail smearing porridge behind it.

"Hugs?" it lisped.

"No hugs," Lizzie said, more certain than ever that she was not a hugger.

"I know that smell," Maddie whispered. "That

used to be the peas porridge in the pot nine days old. No way I'm eating it now."

"No way I was eating it then," said Lizzie.

"Hugs!" it said.

"Hugs?" other voices whispered. The bowls lifted up like half of an oyster shell.

The Porridge Thing kept advancing, its eyes wider, its mouth wetter, and its laugh louder. The girls backed into a wall.

"Do something!" Lizzie shouted to Maddie. "Narrate us out of this!"

"That's not how it works!" Maddie shouted back.

The Porridge began to whimper. "Hugs..."

"Poor thing," Maddie said.

From beneath the clacking bowls, lumps of raisin-studded porridge rolled out, sprouted muddy legs, and began to run. The Porridge squealed with delight and took chase.

"Can't catch me, can't catch me!" the lumps chanted in little gurgles.

The girls edged toward the door through which they had come. Several lumps careened off the ceiling they had been running on and fell splat at their feet.

"Whee!" roared the Porridge Thing, slamming into the door and nearly crushing Maddie in the process. The lumps skittered over Lizzie's foot and the Porridge chased on.

Lizzie reached for the door only to find it had shrunk, the walls puckering around it like a mouth after eating something sour.

"Shrinking potion!" Lizzie shouted. "Give me one now, Maddie!"

Maddie pulled off her hat, rummaging through the contents.

"I don't—" she started, but Lizzie yanked her out of the way of a careening lump. Maddie's hat fell from her hand and rolled away.

Lizzie grabbed the hat and was clipped by a galloping Porridge. Lizzie spun like a top two, three, four times, and came to a dizzy stop. She handed Maddie the hat.

"Right," Lizzie said, eyes angry. "That is about enough of that. You! Table!" she shouted at the furniture shivering against the walls. "Get up!"

The table got up.

"Go there," Lizzie said.

The table started to move.

"Wait!" Lizzie shouted. "Not yet! When I tell you."

One by one, Lizzie addressed every piece of furniture in the room in her most imperious voice, giving them instructions, pointing, and occasionally stamping her foot. After she had relayed her orders, she watched the erratic Porridge chase, held up a finger, and then shouted, "*Now!*"

The tables, chairs, benches, and one wiry little stool trotted to their assigned places.

"A maze!" Maddie shouted. "You made a maze, Lizzie! A-mazing! Hee-hee."

The Porridge chase continued but inside the furniture maze and out of the girls' way.

"Now," Lizzie said, turning to Maddie, "shrinking potion."

"Oh nose, it broke," she said sadly. At her feet lay pieces of glass and several dozen tiny shoes for every occasion. "It spilled on my shoe collection. Now I'll have to make an army of little me-dolls just to keep using them."

"*Ugh!*" Lizzie yelled. "Everything is pell-mell and

mishmash and broken! This is why we need leaders! A good king or queen would rein all this mush in! Someone needs to be in charge!"

"I think the wall agrees with you," Maddie said. "It wiggled when you were talking."

The chandelier began to swing back and forth in a friendly kind of wave.

"The chandelier, too. Hey, maybe the whole school is alive," Maddie said.

"Of course it is," Lizzie said, though she hadn't thought of it till now. "School!" Lizzie shouted upward. "I'm sure you're tired of having impolite and filthy creatures worming about your hallways. Show us the library, and we will fix it for you!"

The walls shuddered, something akin to a laugh or a growl, or perhaps a rumbly intestinal thing that happens after eating some nine-day-old peas porridge. A new door appeared in the wall to their right and opened by itself.

"You could've asked nicer," said Maddie.

"Directness gets results," Lizzie said. There was no time for lollygagging. That peas porridge could escape the maze at any moment, or those greeting card abominations might return. "Watch as we walk comfortably left to right as civil people should."

The two girls entered a low hall. The walls were covered with dusty yellow wallpaper with a complicated black print that moved between shapes like quills and scrolls. As they walked, the patterns in the wallpaper undulated. Lizzie stumbled, her shoe catching on a wrinkle in the carpet. From her half-stooped position, she saw words in the wallpaper. When she stood, they vanished.

"What is it?" Maddie asked, even though she had just narrated it.

"The wallpaper says something," Lizzie said, "but you have to sort of creep along to read it."

Maddie crouched and crept behind Lizzie, reading the words aloud.

"'...blind you can get to the library but only if I guide you must lean against the wall and close your eyes and let it take you place your shoulder here and walk blind you can get to the library but only...' It repeats itself."

"All right, then," said Lizzie. "I'm closing my eyes, School! Take us to the library!"

With eyes closed, they continued their crouched walk. The Narrator could no longer see what Lizzie was doing, but she could hear the rasping noise of her shoulder as it dragged along the wall. On they crept, legs trembling with exhaustion, feeling like a waddling duckling. It might have been fun, if not for the ache in her back and the possibility of a large Wonderlandian monster appearing at any moment to eat them.

Flappy things brushed by them. Their shoes caught on sticky spots. The air turned hot, then cold, then shivery, then scented with ham. Screeches echoed in the distance. At one point, something nipped Maddie on the pinkie of her left hand. She forced her eyes to stay squeezed shut, trusted the school, and kept on.

And then the wall was suddenly gone.

"Um, School?" said Maddie. "Are we there? Or are we facing some kind of unspeakable horror that has eaten the wall?"

"We're there," said Lizzie. "I peeked."

The library had always been a very tall room,

high and narrow windows drizzling light onto eight stories of bookshelves. Now it was even higher and narrower. Lizzie couldn't even see the ceiling, but she could stretch out her hands and touch both walls at the same time. In the narrow space between, books fluttered, hovered, and dived; glided, nested, and cooed. None of the books sat quietly on the shelves where they belonged.

"Hedgehog droppings," Lizzie said.

"There are thousands of books in here," said Maddie. "Maybe millions. Finding the one we want might be imposs—"

"Don't say it," said Lizzie. "Never say that word."

Maddie slapped her hand over her mouth. What was wrong with her? She'd almost said it! And meant it!

Nothing was impossible. Every Wonderlandian knew this from their toenails to their nostrils. And Lizzie more than most. Impossible, it seemed, that she could fulfill her destiny as the next Queen of Hearts. Impossible because she was in exile, her home tainted with bad magic, the way back sealed.

But nothing, nothing, *nothing* is impossible.

Lizzie put her hands on her fists and looked at the books. Looked hard. She remembered a card from her mother about lost things.

♥

Things are never lost to you; you are lost to them.
If ever in need of a Thing that has lost you,
simply stop hiding from it.

♥

She had thought it was a secret message about how to return to Wonderland and had spent several days in obvious locations around the school (Castleteria, roof, front doors), being very Visible and Noisy. But Wonderland hadn't found her, and Lizzie had had to give up when Baba Yaga ordered her to stop scaring the cellar-dwelling baby goblins with all that racket. But maybe allowing a book to find her was the sort of thing her mother was talking about.

"Hello, everyone!" Lizzie shouted, leaping up on a nearby table. "I am Lizzie Hearts. It has come to my attention that there are some Wonderland books that didn't know where I was. Know now.

I am here." She held her arms out, attempting to mimic the inviting gesture Apple did with birds.

The cooing in the shelves paused. The only sound was the rustle of pages as books shifted on their perches. And then one took to the air. Lizzie lifted her hands, and the book landed on her palms. The title read, *Wonderland Through the Ages*.

"Good book," Lizzie whispered.

Then more and more took flight, books landing on Lizzie's head and shoulders, and perching on her arms, pecking the tabletop at her feet, nipping at the hem of her skirt. She resembled Ashlynn Ella in the Enchanted Forest, but instead of being covered in butterflies and pixies, Lizzie was papered with books.

"Here!" Lizzie said, picking one up from the table. "The rest of you are dismissed." She felt again a warm, gooey surge in her middle that was probably something common and unroyal like gratitude. Perhaps her mother wouldn't approve, but Lizzie cleared her throat and added, "Thank you."

The books took to the air with a fluttering of pages and flapping of covers.

"'*Rich Descriptions of Amazing Places for the Curious Agoraphobe*,'" Maddie read. "What's an agoraphobe?"

"I don't know," Lizzie said. "It just seemed right."

She flipped through, finding a chapter describing the Tumtum Grove of Wonderland.

"We should get this to Cedar," Maddie said. "I'm worried we've been gone too long."

Lizzie waved her hand at the comment. "Oh, Kitty isn't *that* irritating. I'm sure she and Cedar have gotten along just fine."

"I meant the Jabberwock," Maddie said. "And it wanting to get us and . . . and my . . ."

Lizzie became aware that Maddie's voice was quavering in the unsettling way that often meant someone was either about to weep or lash out like an army of sharp-toothed and singularly grumpy fairies. Both outcomes were equally unwanted, so Lizzie put a hand on Maddie's shoulder and squeezed softly. She had a speech prepared about the dangers of ill-timed weeping and the awkwardness of fairy violence, but Maddie surprised her by giving her a sudden hug.

"Thanks, Lizzie," Maddie said.

"You're welcome," Lizzie said, that warm gooeyness filling her core. What was happening to her? She let go of Maddie and lifted her chin in the air. "Let's go save the day."

CHAPTER 20

THE VORPAL SWORD AWAITS *Snickersnack!*

CEDAR WOOD WAS STILL SMOOSHING BERRIES and mixing them with oil she'd found in Lizzie's shed. Everything she did was boring.

Kitty Cheshire was still narrating. What was the point? Maddie wasn't missing anything interesting.

Kitty Cheshire decided to make it interesting.

"The paint mixed and ready," Kitty said out loud, "Cedar Wood begins to snuffle around on the ground like a pig looking for truffles."

"I do not!" said Cedar.

"Kitty Cheshire disappears." That part happened. Sometimes this emergency Narrator enjoyed disappearing without reappearing. The in-between-ness felt like bathwater. Like floating. Like being full of soup. "Clearly, Kitty Cheshire had been eaten by the Wonderland Grove Ghost that Cedar Wood knew nothing about. Surely Cedar Wood will be eaten next."

"I can still hear you talking, Kitty."

"Alas, the only thing left of people after having been eaten by the Grove Ghost is their voice, howling with sadness."

"Or howling with madness, in this case."

This game was hexcellent. And distracting. And helped Kitty Cheshire forget the Jabberwock for a few seconds and how even its name stood every hair on her head straight up, and sent tremble-wobbles into her knees, and scared her smile stiff, and how, even though she was far too big now, she longed to curl up on her mother's lap and cry.

Kitty Cheshire regretted thinking those thoughts aloud.

Please come back, Maddie.

Lizzie and Maddie burst through the door,

slamming it shut on what looked to Cedar like thousands of uncomfortably friendly pencils.

"I didn't think-aloud about the pencils," said Kitty. "So that means Maddie is narrating again."

"You're safe!" said Cedar.

"What did I miss?" asked Maddie.

"Boredom," said Kitty. "Talking. Cedar snuffling like a pig."

"I didn't do that!" said Cedar. "Kitty just said I did."

"That's dangerous, Kitty," said Maddie. "I read a story about it in the narration book. Once upon a time there was a Narrator who narrated things that he *didn't* observe, but he was such a powerful and skilled Narrator, the characters actually had to do whatever he said. It was horrible!"

"Like being forced to live out a destiny you don't want?" Cedar muttered under her breath.

"We should get to work," said Maddie. She clasped her gloved hands together. "Hold the spoon, did Madeline Hatter just say, 'We should get to work'?"

"That's nothing," said Kitty. "I was *involved*. I *volunteered* to help." She shuddered again.

"Maddie is correct," said Lizzie. "We don't know how time is moving. We must retrieve the sword and carry it to someone who can wield it, perhaps Headmaster Grimm or Madam Baba Yaga. Surely the White Queen could wield it with panache once she returns."

"So…where's the book?" said Cedar.

Everyone looked at Lizzie. Lizzie sniffed.

"A large crab ate it."

"What?" said Maddie.

"I didn't want to alarm you," said Lizzie, "but one of the flattish stone slabs in the floor of that last hallway was apparently a flattish stone *crab*. It seized the book from my hand with one of its pinchers and devoured it."

"But…but…but…" Maddie couldn't quite seem to talk. The thought of going back through that door made her so nervous the Narrator had difficulty thinking of an appropriate simile. Like she was made of syrup, maybe?

"No matter," said Lizzie. "I read the relevant passage while we were in the library and now have it memorized."

She cleared her throat and recited.

An afternoon in the Tumtum Grove is as warm as a tea party. Tufts of white sillyrose seeds float on the breeze. The spicy scent of primposeys mix with the musky purple odor of the resin dripping from the boles of the Tumtum trees.

Flowers are fond of the Tumtum resin and carpet the ground thicker than grass, drinking it in. The yellow sillyrose on its single, thin stems. The bright blue primposeys with five petals turning up like faces toward the sun. The tiny dots of white snowslips.

The Tumtum trunks are thick and gray, the bark creating long black stripes. Beneath the black soil, roots intertwine. Their canopies touch, branches crissing and crossing so no Tumtum tree stands alone. Their leaves are the size of your palm and perfectly round, and the kind of green that almost sings its color.

In the center of the grove, in the middlemost Tumtum tree, the vorpal sword awaits. Its blade is hidden, thrust into the bole of the tree. Only its crystal hilt sticks out, reflecting the colors of the flowers and waiting to be grasped.

Lizzie continued to recite while Cedar painted on the side of the garden shed, trying to match what Lizzie was describing.

"It's looking almost right," said Lizzie. "But it doesn't *feel* quite right."

"I'm sorry, I'm doing my best," said Cedar.

"To make this painting come alive," said Maddie, "we might need even more than words."

From the shed Lizzie fetched a musical instrument. It was cut from rosewood, shaped like a heart, and strung with thin silver strings.

"I didn't know you played the dulcimer," said Cedar.

Lizzie sniffed. "I don't. Not in public. So I advise you all to keep this performance to yourselves."

Sitting cross-legged on the grass, she placed the dulcimer on her lap. Touching the strings with her left hand and tapping them with a small hammer she held in her right hand, she played a melody that to Cedar's ears sounded strange, somewhat off-key, and yet thickly sweet and oddly beautiful. Maddie felt the song go down her throat like a warm cup of tea and tingle out into her fingers and toes. She didn't mean to cry, but she did. That song was the sound of homesickness.

"Here," said Kitty. She opened a tiny vial that hung from her necklace and held it under Cedar's nose. "This is what Tumtum resin smells like. Cheshires spend a lot of naptime in the branches of Tumtum trees. I brought some resin with me to remind me of home."

The music and the scent filled the Grove, and Cedar painted. Although it was the first time she'd painted with real hands, they still knew how to dip the brush and work it over the wood. She wasn't a wooden girl trying to imitate in paint what was real. She was so real that realness moved out from her and into the paint.

When she lifted her brush and took a step back, Lizzie said, "That's perfect."

"Thanks," said Cedar. She felt alive and unpredictable. What other marvelous things might she be capable of?

"You're different now," Kitty said, "and not just that you're no longer wood."

"I always felt things, even if it was just my imagination," said Cedar. "But I think I was also holding myself back, waiting to be real before I started living."

Lizzie blinked. "You were not real before?"

"Well, my story says I wasn't," said Cedar. "And people like Faybelle always remind me of that."

But her thoughts felt the same in her real head as they had in her wooden head. Had she always been *real* Cedar down to her roots?

"I think this can work," said Maddie, inspecting Cedar's painting. "I *know* it can, in a Narrator-ish way. But only because you're you, Lizzie. Only your hand can claim the sword."

"I am the princess of Hearts," Lizzie declared. "I am an heir to Wonderland! And I command you to give up the vorpal sword."

Lizzie reached her hand toward the painting.

"Careful, the paint is still wet," said Cedar.

But as Lizzie extended her arm, the bumps and imperfections of the wood grain in the shed's boards smoothed and disappeared. Lizzie's hand went through the shed wall—or rather, went into the Tumtum Grove itself as if the painting had created a portal from here to there. Her hand wrapped around the hilt of the vorpal sword, and she yanked. With a wet buzz and a screech of metal, the sword came free.

Lizzie lifted it up, smiling, admiring the warm glow of the blue sword. It appeared to be lighter than Cedar had expected, and just Lizzie's size, too, as if forged for her hand. Lizzie pressed the flat of the blade against her forehead.

"It's beautiful," Lizzie said.

"Isn't it supposed to be purple?" asked Kitty.

"Is it?" said Cedar. "The description didn't say."

With a loud *snap!* the shed wall shuddered, and once again it was just a painting of trees, though now the painted sword was gone and the real sword in Lizzie's hand had turned a bright purple.

"For a minute it was real," said Cedar. She put out her hand but couldn't reach into the Tumtum Grove. She brought back her fingers wet with paint. "So real. And now it's wood again. Wood covered up with pretty paint, dead wood pretending to be...be alive...."

Cedar stopped. Her chin trembled.

The Narrator gave Cedar a hug.

"I wish stories were kinder to their characters," Maddie said. "But I guess trouble is more interesting to read about."

A second shudder—not just the shed this time but the ground beneath their feet. The bubble around the Grove popped. The sky was no longer tinged with yellow but a bright, hot blue. Cedar could see out forever, all the way to the gray stones of the school's towering walls, which were no longer caged by that yellow dome.

"The Jabberwock," Maddie whispered. "It broke the magical barrier."

She remembered the great beast hurling itself at the barrier, clawing at the magic, trying to smash through. Maybe frustrated that it couldn't find the Wonderlandians in the school, it had turned its attention again to that other Wonderlandian it had sensed: the Mad Hatter.

Maddie started to run. She didn't turn back to observe if the other girls were coming, too, as a good Narrator should. She was thinking about her dad, and how he made her charm blossom tea when she was confused and lavender tea when she was too happy to fall asleep, and how he was always smiling around those huge teeth that didn't seem to quite fit in his mouth. He was the silliest person in the world, and she loved him more than hats and tea and hopping combined.

Maddie fled the Grove and raced toward the school, watching the sky.

"If the Jabberwock gets to Book End, that'll be it," Cedar said, running from behind Maddie. "The story will be over. No chance to undo the magic. Raven always a raven, Apple always an apple, and—"

"We know! Silence!" Lizzie said, but she sounded more worried than angry.

"Where are the teachers?" said Cedar. "Madam Baba Yaga! Headmaster Grimm! We have the vorpal sword! Come get it and take care of the Jabberwock!"

"There they are!" said Lizzie.

Just over the rise, the green grass of the croquet field near the school had changed to perfect squares of black and white. Cedar could see the silhouettes of Headmaster Grimm, Baba Yaga, and a handful of other faculty members. Why were they holding so still?

"Curiouser and curiouser..." Kitty whispered, her sharp eyes picking up what the others could not yet see.

The girls stopped on the rise. The teachers were still as marble. As stone. As giant chess pieces on the chessboard lawn.

The Jabberwock had broken the barrier. Its magic was spreading.

"No," Cedar whispered.

And then the Jabberwock itself arrived.

As one, the four girls dropped flat to the ground behind some rosebushes. The thorns grazed Cedar's arms, leaving thin red scratches.

The wind made by the Jabberwock's great wings knocked over several of the faculty chess pieces as it hovered over them, sniffing the air. Wherever its shadow grazed, plants turned to paper, grass turned to chessboards, benches ran away, rocks popped and stones deflated, and the world turned mad.

"But we have the sword," Cedar said sadly. "The teachers were supposed to use it and defeat the...the—"

And then the Jabberwock took off faster than Cedar had thought possible. Directly toward them.

"Don't see us, don't see us, don't see us," Maddie muttered.

Don't see us, don't see us....

The Jabberwock passed over their heads. It landed heavily in the Grove, sinking its claws into the grass. It inhaled. The color was sucked out of the plants. Trees wilted. Flowers turned gray as ashes. Grass dried up. The Jabberwock was sucking the Wonder out of the Grove.

Lizzie made a heartbreaking strangled sound. Maddie put her hand over Lizzie's mouth.

The Jabberwock's head swiveled in their direction, its huge gray nostrils sniffing. And Cedar knew it was over. They were about to become buttered bandersnatches.

A shout.

"Halloo! Halloo!"

Someone was running across the Troll Bridge from Book End, directly toward the Jabberwock, and waving his arms. Trying to get the beast's attention away from the girls shivering inside the bushes.

"No, Dad," Maddie said.

"Halloo and yoohoo!" called the Mad Hatter. "Nothing for you there, beastie! Come have a spot of tea with me!"

The Jabberwock took to the air and zoomed toward the Hatter. Maddie got up to run to him, to put herself between her father and the monster.

Kitty grabbed Maddie. "I know what you're planning to do. I can hear your narration. But you can't stop it now. Stay down."

"What's he doing?" Maddie said. "The Jabber-wock will take him, too, and—"

"He's trying to keep the Jabberwock both away from us and out of Book End, to keep the story going," said Kitty.

The beast nose-dived at the Mad Hatter, picked him up with a clawed foot, and swooped away from Book End and back toward the school. It went straight through a wall, the stones toppling easily, falling lightly and soundlessly to the ground like empty gift boxes.

Maddie realized all three girls were holding her, hugging her. If they hadn't been, she was certain she would have forgotten how to keep standing up and fallen to the ground. She had to keep observing, keep narrating, now more than ever, or the story would end with her dad captured by that monster.

"What about the other faculty?" said Cedar. "The

ones on the field trips to the East, West, and South Winds. They'll return soon. Right?"

Cedar madly tapped at her MirrorPhone, but the spreading of the Jabberwock magic had knocked them out-of-area again.

Maddie shook her head. She was struggling with yet another unfamiliar sensation: annoyance. Just where were all those responsible adults who should have been taking care of things like terrifying magically mad beasts that want to rearrange reality and steal your dad and transform your best friend into a bird and ruin an otherwise lovely afternoon?

Lizzie was staring back at the ruined Grove, her arms dangling at her sides, the sword dragging in the dirt.

When she turned, her expression was hard as boiled eggs.

"We do not need the teachers. We survived here with the broken things, the crooked things, the things Jabberwocked and gibbering. Time cannot be wasted waiting for them to return, when they'll just be turned into chess pieces. That creature took Maddie's dad and stole away our friends. The longer a thing is not what it is, the more likely it will forget the thing that it was before. The Jabberwock must be stopped."

"What do we do?" asked Cedar.

Lizzie held up the sword. "We take off its head."

CHAPTER 21

BEWARE EMPATHY!

Danger! Danger!

IZZIE'S HEART HURT. IT FELT WOUNDED IN there, barely pumping, as wilted and colorless as the beautiful plants of her Grove.

And that made Lizzie Hearts, who was already quite mad, even madder.

She stormed through the heart-shaped door with Maddie, Kitty, and Cedar on her heels. They were not greeted with bottom-of-the-well decor, restless furnishings, or shouting greeting cards, but with a simple white room with one normalish door and one dark purple carpeted opening that was door-sized.

The normalish door bore a sign scribbled in orange crayon: JABBERWOCK NOT THROUGH HERE.

"That is not a trustworthy scrawl," Lizzie said. "Someone may be trying to trick us into not taking the correct door."

"Or someone may be trying to trick us into thinking they are tricking us, making us choose the trick door by saying it isn't what it is," said Kitty.

"Stop saying 'trick!'" Lizzie shouted. "I'm tired of that word!"

The shouting hadn't cured her knee-tremble and belly-twistiness as she'd hoped. Lizzie gripped the sword hilt harder. That Jabberwock would pay for what it did to her Grove.

She turned back to the "trick" door (sorry, Lizzie), only to discover it missing, replaced with an empty wall.

"Did one of you steal the door?" Lizzie asked.

"Not me," Maddie said.

"Me neither," Kitty said.

The three girls looked at Cedar expectantly.

"Um . . . no?" she said. "I didn't even know stealing doors was an option."

And then the wall sort of blinked and the door they had come through was also gone.

"Aha!" Lizzie said. "Unless one of you is lying, *Cedar*, the school itself is stealing doors."

"The school must want us to go that way," Maddie said.

"Forward! Into the purple fur hole!" Lizzie said, then added, "*So there!*" because shouting did make her fluttery-tummy and noodley-knees feel a tiny bit stronger.

Tendrils of long purple carpet tickled Lizzie's face and whispered against her arms as she scampered through the opening. But despite the grapeish furriness, the tunnel felt welcoming, exhaling a cool, fresh breeze.

"It's too easy," Lizzie said.

Cedar looked around nervously. "It's also quiet, maybe *too* quiet. You think something is waiting to surprise us, or eat us, or something?"

"I hope so," Lizzie said, patting the sword. She tightened her lips and lifted her chin to look braver.

The purple-carpeted tunnel ended, spilling them onto the polished wooden planks of the

Grimmnasium. At the far end of the huge room sprawled the lumpy, scaled shape of a beast. The school had brought them directly to the Jabberwock.

"Thanks, Ever After High," Maddie whispered, petting the wall.

The Jabberwock was using its clawed, three-toed paws to attach something to its head, but the Narrator couldn't bear to describe it.

"It's Maddie's dad!" Lizzie whisper-shouted. "The thing is tying the Mad Hatter to its head with vines and sealing wax! It's making the Mad Hatter into a hat—a Wonder-powered hat at that."

Maddie felt trembly. "We need to save him."

The Jabberwock made a jerky movement, and the girls pressed themselves back into the shag-carpeted walls. Lizzie hid the vorpal sword behind her back.

"Just as soon as I cut off its head," she whispered.

She was certainly mad enough to do it, but just how did one go about slaying a beast that big?

The creature began to wiggle its hindquarters back and forth, patting its head as if showing off its Mad Hatter hat to an imaginary crowd of admirers.

"We have to save Maddie's dad *first*!" Cedar whispered.

The beast picked something long and stringy from between its two enormous front teeth.

"This is my destiny," said Lizzie. "This foul beast is of Wonderland. Wonderland out of order. And my story is a story of order. I will march right up to the beast and sever its wretched head from its shoulders with one swift swing of the vorpal sword! Maybe two."

"What if you miss?" Maddie asked in a quiet voice. "What if your swing is off or if the Jabberwock moves? What if you hit my dad?"

"I won't miss," Lizzie said, and Maddie's gaze dropped. Cedar looked nervous. Kitty was trembling so hard she looked a little blurry. Hardly the enthusiasm she'd expect in the middle of her rousing battle speech.

"Imagine something," Cedar said. "Imagine that's your dad up there."

Lizzie imagined. Her wonderlandiful dad. A tiny man in a huge crown and an impractical grin. Stuck on a monster's head. And someone else swinging a sword about. And Lizzie understood.

♥

Beware Empathy! Empathy forces you to Understand how others are feeling and to Care! Danger! Danger!

♥

But it was too late. Lizzie had Imagined. Lizzie had Empathized. And now Lizzie *Cared*.

"Of course we'll free him first," said Lizzie. "By the jack of spades we will. After all, we are the Wonder Worms."

Maddie smiled at her. Lizzie smiled back and wondered if empathy wasn't quite as bad as her mother believed.

CHAPTER 22

~~HEDGEHOG~~ ~~CROQUET~~ BATTLE!

ET'S GET ON WITH THE DAD-SAVING, THEN, so I can slay this beast," said Lizzie.

"Wait," said Cedar. "What happens when the Jabberwock dies?"

"Its magic will be undone," said Maddie. "Hopefully."

"All its magic?"

Cedar pressed a hand to her chest and felt that violent beating of her heart that meant she was scared. But also alive.

Wait, Cedar wanted to say again, but she knew they couldn't wait. She *could* still save herself, outrun the Jabberwock and its magic and the changing-back, go home, and stay real forever after....

"I'm guessing we've got about twenty seconds before the Jabberwock notices us," Kitty said. She stood the farthest back of all of them, pressed into the purple shag. "If you can manage to get all your fretting and questioning out before then..."

Cedar took a deep breath, air filling her up. She was no longer "cursed" with kindness. So this is who Cedar really was. The kind of girl who did not run away. Who faced the monster. Who said, "How dare you hurt my friends? Prepare to feel the wrath of the puppet."

A hand squeezed hers, and Cedar squeezed back. There was a lot of comfort in knowing that the Narrator was on her side.

The Narrator, meanwhile, was avoiding describing the Jabberwock and the sad parody of a hat upon its brow. The Narrator did not comment on how this made her feel, as that is not something

Narrators do. But Maddie put a hand over her trembling chin and tried very hard not to fall apart.

The Jabberwock was sniffing the rosebush that used to be Briar. The roses bent and tugged by its inhale, and the entire bush began to quiver. The Jabberwock opened its huge maw as if to take a bite.

"No," Cedar whispered.

"Beast!" Lizzie ran into the Grimmnasium. "Step away from the irritating bush! You've destroyed enough plants today!"

The Jabberwock swung its head around, its white-blind eyes fiery now, looking right at them.

Kitty went semitransparent.

"Thoughtful—" the Jabberwock skurbled.

"Yes, I am," Lizzie interrupted. "Now, remove your hat and present your neck for chopping, or it will go badly for you."

The Jabberwock dropped to its stomach and used its legs to slide itself forward, and continued, "—to trawl me up a Wonderling three-batch for squeezing."

Its voice was low and raspy, and shrieked into

Cedar's ears the way fingernails scratching chalk-boards do. Surely it hadn't yet recognized the sword in Lizzie's hands, as it seemed unworried, playful, spinning itself around on its stomach.

"Why is it doing that creepy walk?" Kitty whispered from the purple tunnel. "I don't like it, I don't like it. . . ."

The Mad Hatter had slumped over on its head, visibly breathing but limp with exhaustion, and the Jabberwock pulsed with a pale sickly light. Strengthened and fearless, it was leaching the Hatter's Wonder.

"Kitty, transport yourself onto it, untie Maddie's dad, and then vanish yourselves away," Lizzie whispered back at them.

Kitty turned fully invisible. "I'm not good with knots," she peeped.

"*Wee-wee meaty food-legs, food-legs, food-legs*," the Jabberwock sang, slithering closer. It was nearly upon them.

"Kitty . . ."

"I can't I can't I can't . . ." Kitty whispered from the air.

"Fine, scaredy-cat," Lizzie said. "I will distract it, and *Cedar* will save the Mad Hatter."

"Me?" Cedar was supposed to be the girl who was quiet and friendly and painted pictures. In the stories, Pinocchio never slew a dragon.

"Prepare to face the wrath of the puppet," she whispered, trying to give herself courage.

"I said your neck, slivy creature!" Lizzie was shouting.

"Neck?" it grinkled, backing toward her. "All is inside out. Upside down. Leftways right. Front-wards back. Here is my neck." It batted its tail sassily.

"That's just too disturbing," Kitty whispered.

The Jabberwock poked Lizzie in the belly with the tip of its tail. She swung the sword and missed. Its tail continued to poke, pat her head, slap her cheek, nudge her in the ribs.

"Stop it!" Lizzie shouted, awkwardly swiping the sword, touching nothing but air.

The beast began chittering like a giant chorus of drowning crickets.

"There is no laughing at your future monarch!" Lizzie hollered.

"Go," whispered Kitty, giving Cedar a nudge. "Now's your chance. I'll…er…keep a lookout."

Cedar crept forward, achingly aware that she was no longer made of nice, safe, painless wood.

The frightened and confused thoughts spilling out of Cedar helped distract the Narrator from what was truly terrifying: her father, strapped to a monster's head. The Narrator had to stay focused. If she stopped narrating, the story would stop, and her father would never escape.

"Please help him," Maddie whispered.

"If I have to work my way back-end forward, so be it!" said Lizzie.

She swung the sword recklessly at the tail in her face and managed to snip off an inch.

The creature roared. It spun around with startling speed. Cedar scrabbled out of its way. But Lizzie just stood and stared at a small opening in the air the sword had left behind, as if the air was just fabric, and the vorpal sword had sliced it open. Lizzie's eyes widened, peering through the slice till it snapped shut.

The Jabberwock turned around completely and slammed down a taloned paw. Lizzie only just managed to dodge it, rolling across the floor with the force and slamming into Cedar.

The monster began to do a cheeky dance, making that horrible, fingernails-on-chalkboard kind of raspy chuckle.

"I don't know how to save Maddie's dad," Cedar said, splayed on the floor beside Lizzie.

"Saving things. This is not normally my specialty," Lizzie said, crawling to her feet.

A toddler-sized furball in a fetching white jacket burst through the double doors at the opposite end of the Grimmnasium.

"*Grra-ha!*" Daring-beastie announced. It charged the Jabberwock and was swatted unceremoniously aside by the beast's tail.

"That's Daring!" said Cedar. "And saving things *is* his specialty."

"Good," Lizzie said. "I will keep distracting." She yelled as she ran at the Jabberwock, who kept dancing away, whiffling and burbling as if enjoying itself tremendously.

Cedar and Maddie helped Daring-beastie to his feet. Earl Grey popped out of Maddie's hat and squeaked emphatically, pointing at the Jabberwock with a hat pin. Earl Grey was a mouse, but he had no problem imagining himself as a hero.

You spent your entire life imagining emotions, smells, textures, Cedar thought. *Imagine yourself a hero now.*

Daring-beastie searched around frantically. "*Groooard*," he howled, asking for a sword.

From across the room Lizzie threw something that clanged to the floor at Daring-beastie's feet. It was an ornate butter knife with a beautifully engraved heart on the handle.

Daring-beastie brandished the butter knife.

"*Squeak?*" Earl Grey asked.

"*Squeak!*" Daring said, pointing at Maddie's dad.

Cedar squared her shoulders. She imagined herself: fearless, bold, powerful. Successful.

"Let's do this," Cedar said. "With fuzzy help."

"*Groar!*" said Daring.

Cedar and her furry friends tried to climb up the monster's leg, but it was moving around too fast in its odd sideways crawl. Staying in the Jabberwock's blind spot, she gestured at Lizzie, trying to tell her they needed help.

Lizzie was swinging the vorpal sword, taunting, "I'll chop you up like salad! Like a really big, nasty salad no one wants to eat! Not even vegetarians! Or…especially not vegetarians! Ah-ha!"

"A walking joke is thee, me wee heartspawn." The Jabberwock hissed, breathing magic on her so powerful her crown melted into golden icicles. "Hee-hee-saw."

"My crown!" Lizzie hollered. "I had hoped to spare my little friends this, but *you* deserve it." She raised her sword. "Hedgehogs! To your princess!"

A chittering *roink* heralded the sound of a hedgehog moving at an incredible speed. It darted across the Grimmnasium floor and stopped solidly in front of Lizzie.

Lizzie held the sword like a croquet mallet and swung, striking the hedgehog hard with the flat of the sword. The hedgehog flew, straight and true, directly into the snout of the approaching beast, quills burying themselves in its soft nose. The Jabberwock froze as if stunned.

Cedar took advantage of the Jabberwock's momentary stillness and boosted Daring-beastie up, climbing after him and Earl Grey. She was expecting skin like a snake's or a lizard's, but the Jabberwock's hide was slick as jelly and left pads of stickiness on her fingertips.

Thunk! A hedgehog struck the Jabberwock's shoulder and stuck. The little beast smiled at Cedar as she tiptoed up the monster's ridged back.

I'm light as a leaf, Cedar thought, trying to imagine it to be true. *I'm as bendable as a branch. I fly like a seedpod. I tear my way through problems like an oak's deepest root through rock. I am a hero.*

From her art tools pouch in her pocket, she pulled her pencil-sharpening knife. It was the very one that had sliced her newly real fingertip. Did that only happen a few hours ago? It felt like years. She joined Earl Grey and Daring-beastie, slicing at the vines.

Finally free, the Mad Hatter slumped into her arms, snoring softly. He was sometimes a small man, but it looked like he'd been playing with the grow potions again and was tall and thin. Cedar could barely hold him. How to get down?

"I got him," a mouth said in front of her,

expanding into all of Kitty Cheshire. She took the Mad Hatter in her shaking arms and quickly disappeared with the unconscious man, reappearing to lay him down near Maddie and the purple tunnel. Daring-beastie and Earl Grey leaped away.

"Maneuver C," Lizzie said from below. She broke a golden icicle from her melted crown and tossed it on the floor.

Shuffle, the last hedgehog left in Lizzie's armory, picked up the icicle with her tiny pink hands, nodded, and curled up into a ball. Swift and strong, Lizzie slapped the hedgehog with the flat of the blade, and the little beast stuck right between the Jabberwock's eyes.

Shuffle poked it in the eye with the icicle, the Jabberwock roared, and Cedar was violently bucked off.

Light as a leaf, Cedar thought, and fell, landing on her back.

Ouch. There was pain but not as much as she'd feared. She sat up and realized why. Daring-beastie had leaped to her rescue, attempting to catch her but mostly just breaking her fall. He gave her a fuzzy thumbs-up.

Cedar had only just gotten to her knees when the Jabberwock noticed her. Its head swung around on a giant snakelike neck, fiery eyes inches from her face. Its huge nose snuffled her. If not for the cheerful icicle-waving hedgehog affixed between the creature's eyes, Cedar was sure she would have starting crying, or screaming, or both. The enormous mouth opened and exhaled over her. Its breath was hot and cold at once and stunk of wet dog and burned turnips. The breath magic was so strong it rustled Cedar's clothes and changed them into paper, her dress now made of stitched-together pages ripped out of a book about Pinocchio.

"The game's score is Wonderling naught," the Jabberwock gargled. "Why does the bitsy play-squeal not change?"

Daring-beastie was punching the Jabberwock in the neck, but the Jabberwock didn't budge.

"Why?" it insisted, its bucktoothed mouth leering over her. "Wordspew! Tell my greatness why you normal stay and change not!"

Lie, Cedar thought. She could say she was magic, beyond its power, poisonous to eat, destined to slay a Jabberwock, anything to scare it and make it leave her alone.

But Cedar chose to tell the truth. "I *am* changed," she said, her voice quavering. "But it's wrong, like all your changes. Right now, I'm supposed to be made of wood. I've got little brass pegs on my joints, and I don't feel pain or breathe, and I can only tell the truth. One day the Blue-Haired Fairy might turn me into a real girl forever after. But it's not my time yet."

"A lie," the beast said, pointing one claw at her. "A most ridiculish lie."

Lizzie had crept up to its neck, and now she swung. The vorpal sword went *snickersnack*.

Hearing for the first time the telltale noise of the vorpal sword, the Jabberwock jerked away just before the sword reached its neck. It reared its head, knocking Lizzie. The sword flew out of her hands, and she landed several feet away.

"Lizzie!" Cedar said, running to her.

"Where is the sword?" Lizzie whispered.

The Jabberwock was staring at the shimmering trail the sword had cut in the air.

"Vorpal!" sloared the Jabberwock. "*Vor*paaaal!"

"*Grrrr...ha!*" Daring-beastie growled, reaching the sword first. He lifted it up, struggling with the weight.

All sassiness and patience melted from the Jabberwock. It charged Daring-beastie, who suddenly vanished. The Jabberwock skidded to a halt, sniffing the air, smelling the lemony trail of Kitty's disappearance. Several feet away, the Daring-beastie reappeared, the sword floating beside him as if it had a life of its own. And then the sword vanished.

"Vorpal!" scrackled the Jabberwock, mad with rage.

A *snickersnack* sounded from the far end of the Grimmnasium. Kitty was perched atop the basketball standard.

"So much moving around," she said, swinging the sword. "It's really draining to carry oth—"

Whatever Kitty was going to say was lost as she stared at the hole in the air her swing had cut. She smiled, baring each of her Cheshire teeth.

"Guys!" she said, her voice actually bubbly.

"This sword can get us home! That's Wonderland in there." She pointed at the hole as it snapped shut. "Who cares if it's infected or something. So is Ever After currently. Let's just—"

The Jabberwock clawed a wooden board from the floor and threw it across the length of the basketball court, impaling the backboard and sending the whole standard crashing to the floor.

"Kitty!" Cedar yelled.

The Jabberwock galloped to the mess, screaming, "*Vorpaaaal!*"

"We could...*ugh*...use that beast on the Ever After High basketball team," Kitty whispered from behind Cedar.

Cedar whirled. "You're okay!"

Kitty coughed. "Relatively." Her eyes were half-lidded and her ear was bleeding a little. "Vanishing, moving, vanishing...it takes a lot out of you. Especially when you carry stuff."

The Jabberwock was picking through the broken standard bits with its claws and mouth, searching. "*Swoooord,*" it howled.

"You do the honors, princess," Kitty said, holding

up the sword. "Forget this monster. Use the sword to open a door home."

"No!" said Cedar. "What about Ever After? You can't just leave the Jabberwock here!"

"I *could* go home," Lizzie mused. "Raise an army, come back, take over—"

"What?" Cedar said. "Like the Evil Queen, but in reverse?"

Lizzie's eyes cleared from whatever daydream she was in. "Of course not."

The creature in question had given up searching the rubble for the sword. Cedar heard its claws clicking on the hardwood, coming back toward them.

"Give me the sword, Kitty," Lizzie said. "Quick!"

"Only if you promise to take us home," said Kitty, taking a step back.

"Cat Thing!" came a terrible screech from above.

With great flaps of its bat wings, the Jabberwock leaped and descended upon them in a crash. Everyone went flying, but especially Kitty. Cedar saw her spinning almost to the ceiling. The sword flew out of her hand, singeing the air with a narrow rip. The sword struck the wall, careened back, and began to descend into the tear it had made. Midair, Kitty reached for it.

They would both plunge back into Wonderland. It was over, Cedar thought. The sword would be gone.

Kitty popped out of thin air, dropping the vorpal sword at Lizzie's feet.

"She caught it," Cedar said. "Before it fell into Wonderland."

"And came back to us before *she* did," Maddie said.

"Off with its head, Your Highness," Kitty said, her eyes closing. She curled into a ball. "Just going to take a little catnap..."

Lizzie patted Kitty's head and picked up the sword. Her beautiful crown hung in broken golden icicles. The painted heart around her left eye was smeared. Her skirt was ripped; her tights bore ragged holes in the knees. But her eyes were clear and her mouth was set.

She raised the sword. "Now, Shuffle!"

The Jabberwock opened its mouth as if to eat Lizzie, but Lizzie's pet, still stuck between the monster's eyes, tossed the golden icicle into the creature's throat.

"*Hurrg!*" gagged the Jabberwock.

"I'm glad you're on our side, Princess of Hearts," said Cedar.

"Callooh callay," said Lizzie. "It's about to become a frabjous day."

CHAPTER 23

A RULER OF

~~NOTHING~~ Wonderland

IZZIE SWUNG THE SWORD, MISSING WILDLY. A huge scaly paw swatted her for the trouble, and she went skidding to the ground.

She leaped up, irritated. It was not supposed to be like this. It was her *destiny* to bring Wonderland to heel, but her Grove was destroyed and everyone was hurt. Lizzie probed her swollen lip. *She* was hurt, for queen's sake! The only one hurt was supposed to be the Jabberwock, and apart from the smiling hedgehog wedged between its eyes, the beast was suffering from nothing more than a golden icicle stuck in its gullet.

"*Hork*," gagged the Jabberwock, holding up a claw to Lizzie as if it were in the middle of a speech and just needed her to wait a moment.

"Get him, Lizzie!" Maddie shouted, almost back to her usual happy self.

"Is your dad okay, then?" Lizzie asked. Empathy filled her, but instead of causing indigestion, she actually felt amazing. Maybe her mother was wrong about a few things. What a terrifying thought! Lizzie ordered it to the back of her head to inspect later. "Never mind. He's off the head, so I'm killing it now!"

Lizzie charged the Jabberwock and swung, just managing to take off the tip of a horn before being kicked away. Oh, spades take it. Maybe all this empathy was throwing off her aim.

"*Hurk*," said the Jabberwock, still working on expelling the hedgehog-flung icicle from its insides.

Maddie took off her shoe, shouted "Hatworm is go!" and threw it at the Jabberwock.

"I don't need any help!" Lizzie shouted. "I'm trying to fulfill my destiny, and you're messing me up!"

"*Hurglaaa!*"

The Jabberwock finally coughed out the icicle, the force expelling it straight at Lizzie. Fast.

"*Shrunk*" was the sound that Lizzie heard as the golden icicle struck her.

How curious, Lizzie thought, even as the pain blossomed, *that the sound of a coughed-up golden icicle glancing across one's forehead would sound like an actual word that has nothing to do with icicles, gold, or foreheads.* Her legs weakened, and she dropped to one knee. *I shall have to tell Maddie about it. Also, apologize for being so curt.*

"Lizzie!" Maddie was leaning over her. Lizzie couldn't think of the last time anyone had been so close to her. Besides her hedgehog, Shuffle, of course. But she didn't really count as an anyone because of all the spiky fur. Lizzie preferred pets that weren't too soft.

"I wanted to tell you…something," Lizzie slurred.

"I know," Maddie said, grabbing her arm. "I already narrated it."

"*Rrraaaagggh!*" roared the Jabberwock. It had Cedar trapped against a wall. A torrent of its transforming breath blasted her. The pages of Cedar's paper dress yellowed and curled at the edges.

"If the playsqueal meat will not tweak into something yummier," the Jabberwock skrittled, "'twill be simpler just to eat as is!"

"Absolutely not!" Lizzie yelled, wobbling to her feet. "That girl is under the protection of the Court of Wonderland. Any action against her will be considered high treason!"

The Jabberwock lifted one feathery eyebrow. "Hee! I see no Wonderland! We stand on Else. *My* Else. The Heartspawn is a ruler of nothing."

"Wherever I am, *there* is Wonderland," said Lizzie, sure of it now. "A queen carries her kingdom always."

The fiend chuckled, flapping its claws around in a gesture meant to take in everything. "The Wonder here was wrought by Jabberwock. Seemings that where ere *I* am, there is the Land of Wonder."

"This is *not* Wonderland!" Lizzie said. "This is an abomination. A corruption. A poison. Your eyes are no longer fiery, which means you used up all the energy you stole from the Mad Hatter. You are getting weaker, and *I* wield the vorpal sword."

"The sword sings strong," the Jabberwock gurgled. "But a shoddy conductor are thee. You swipeswipeswipe and murder only air. Little missmissmiss could nary hope to sever this greatness of neck. And alas and alack, as the poem smacks, 'tis the *only* way to defeat me. But to finish off tiny girlings, my Wonder-less paws are terror enough."

It launched itself at Lizzie, clawed paws out.

Lizzie, with muscles hardened by years of swinging flamingos and hurling hedgehogs, swung the sword with all the might, rage, and sovereign right she could muster, and parted the Jabberwock from an entire paw. A ripple in the air opened, and the paw dropped through. The hole snapped closed.

The great beast roared, and Lizzie smiled. *Now* it was hurt. It skittered away, pulling its wounded arm close.

Lizzie pulled on the hilt, but her colossal blow had buried the tip of the sword several inches into the floor.

Maddie rushed forward to help Lizzie free the sword. The Jabberwock whirled, still cradling its arm, but a tiny pink replacement paw was already sprouting from the wound.

"Hey, Jabberwocky!" Cedar yelled. She raced around, picking up odd balls and loose floorboards, throwing them at the beast, trying to distract it from Lizzie and Maddie. "That sword opens doors to Wonderland. Don't you want to go home, where there are real, tasty bandersnatches?"

A bit of longing passed through the Jabberwock's eyes. But it lowered its wet gray eyelids and scowled. "In Wonderland I am endgame of the Galumphing Hunt. It is destiny rhyme-declared. But here the election is mine. Here I will be *king*! Once vorpal is mine."

The Jabberwock glared at Lizzie and Maddie, who were tugging desperately on the sword. It pulled its tail back for a mighty blow.

"Hold on," Maddie said.

"I will," Lizzie said, and kicked Maddie away from the tail whipping toward them. "Keep telling the sto—"

And then, pain. Lizzie didn't think she had ever felt so ouchy. The impact lifted her off her feet even as it knocked the sword free from the floor. She was sliding sideways and half upside down, spinning past the Jabberwock, but she managed to keep hold of the hilt. The sword trailed dark lines through the air. She saw her fingers loosen on the grip and commanded them to stop, to tighten, to hold firm, to keep tearing an opening in the air. It would have to be enough.

At last the sword fell from her numb fingers and dropped into the hole it had made.

Lizzie struck the far wall and slid to the floor, the breath knocked out of her. The doorway the sword had torn was huge, tracing the entire path from where Lizzie had been struck to where she landed.

A scaly paw dipped into the divide and caught the sword.

"There, then, and now," the Jabberwock said with a bucktoothed, scaly smile. "My paws belong around such as this."

The hutling crashed into the Grimmnasium, front door/mouth open, coughing its student contents out. A raven dropped an apple on the monster's head, caught it, and flew away. The Jabberwock stumbled back, its rear paws slipping on a golden lock and a brass egg. It attempted to steady itself with the clawed hand that did not hold the sword, and managed to cut that paw on an ax held up by a tree.

The Jabberwock roared as it tripped and tipped into the shrinking portal to Wonderland. Lizzie was certain the opening would snap shut on the beast and banish its top half back to its home world. But the Jabberwock brought the sword up, the flat of the blade sparking against the edge of the opening, forcing it slowly back open. The monster wasn't falling. The hole wasn't closing. The rip was like an open wound between worlds, the Jabberwock the infection keeping it from healing.

"You can't stay here," Lizzie shouted at it. "Ever After is home to the kind, and the friendly, and the brave, and you are none of those things!"

"Are you?" the Jabberwock scrissed.

It wrapped its tail around her ankle, and its eyes began to pulse a bright unsettling white. Lizzie felt energy sap out of her with each pulse, the *Wonder* draining from her bones. Shuffle, the last hedgehog remaining affixed to the Jabberwock, dropped off the creature and scuttled to Lizzie's side, nuzzling her with her spikes.

"This world is mine!" the Jabberwock skreamled.

Lizzie couldn't seem to sit up. She could barely catch her breath, but she managed to whisper, "Hatworm is go...."

Okay, Lizzie. Okay. I will finish this. Somehow.

CHAPTER 24

MADNESS IS LIFE

THE JABBERWOCK HAD THE SWORD. LIZZIE was lying, hurt, on the floor. The Narrator was new at this, but she was certain an Ever After story should not end with the monster victorious. But she'd taken an oath to never, ever, ever interfere. It was an impossible thing.

Then again, she wasn't only the Narrator. She was also Madeline Hatter. And Maddie imagined six impossible things before breakfast.

"You should go home," Maddie said.

The Jabberwock still held the rip between two

worlds open with the sword, as if deciding which one to conquer first.

"Pardon beg?" it asked.

"There's no pardon for what you've done here," said Maddie. "The best I can do is send you home."

"*You*," bellowed the Jabberwock, "send *me* home? Are you a girl-prince? Nay. A sword-swinger? Nay. Hatted thing stands around, letting other meatlings play while you watch. You are a sillypants of terrible degree."

"Thank you," Maddie said. She could see ripples of color and light through the tear. Wonderland was sick, but it was still beautiful. Scents rolled out—the sparkling zest of Tumtum trees, the cool crackle of broken water, the sharp oyster tang of the air. "You should be fizz-bobbled and glee-sprinkled to go to Wonderland. I would be."

The Jabberwock began its horrible, chittering laugh. Laugh? At Wonderland? Maddie clenched her teeth and decided to break some rules.

"The Jabberwock pushed against the edge of the tear, and it widened," Maddie said.

And it happened, just as she'd narrated.

The Jabberwock goggled the widening tear.

"What magic is this?" it bellowed.

"Storytelling," Maddie said.

The Jabberwock gnashed its teeth. "No puppet am I. Especially of a Tiny. Hatted. Girl."

"Hey!" said Maddie. "I count a puppet as a heart-twinned friend. You should be so lucky."

It pulled out the sword and advanced on Maddie.

The tear began to close behind it.

"Until it didn't," Maddie said quickly. "Until the tear between worlds stopped closing, waiting for one more important thing to pass through."

At her words, the closing of the tear did slow down, but it did not stop completely.

The Jabberwock's eyes pulsed white. "The Nothing in you echoes. I will claim your leftover Wonder. The Hat Girl is an empty shell."

Maddie sagged. She did feel empty and tired.

The Jabberwock towered over Maddie, the stink of its breath ruffling her hair.

"Whatever telling-story spark you have stolen is not enough. My will is strongest. My power law. You serve me now."

"That's it," Maddie whispered, smiling. "I made an oath to serve the story and the reader and no other, be it king or queen or baker or candlestick maker. Or Jabberwock."

"Mufflewords." The Jabberwock rumbled above her, saliva dripping from its lips. "Clearspeak now. Loudly."

Maddie straightened. "You're right. My power is not enough. But their power is."

The Jabberwock snaked its head around, scanning the destruction it had wrought in the Grimmnasium, and found nothing it considered a threat. "Whose power?"

"Theirs," Maddie said, pointing at you. Yes, you. The ones reading this book. "I'm only half the storyteller. The Readers are the other half. After all, they take the words and make the pictures in their minds—make the story *real*. Isn't that right, Readers?"

Feel free to nod, say yes or darn tootin' or absotively, or whatever feels just right.

The Jabberwock took a step back. "Brainfraught babbletalk! You are mad!"

Maddie smiled. "Why, yes, I believe I am! And you want to know a secret, little Wocking Jay?" Her voice dropped to a hush, and she leaned closer to the monster. "Madness is life."

Okay, Readers, help me. Think the words aloud. Or say them aloud. Narrate it to be true.

"Go home, Jabberwock," said Maddie.

Go home, Jabberwock. A chorus of unseen voices repeated her words from across time, space, and the wiggly bits in between.

Three times more, Readers!

Go home.

Go home!

GO HOME!

The great fiend that is the Jabberwock, terror of two worlds and bane of bandersnatches, stumbled backward, pushed by voices it heard suddenly, powerfully, shouting in its own mind.

"NO!" it roared.

The tear widened, a monstrous mouth tall and wide, shimmering around the edges, brilliant with the light of Wonderland. The Jabberwock thrashed, but its head dipped into the hole.

"Yes," Maddie said.

"Impossible!" it screeched, its body tumbling through.

Maddie laughed. "Nothing is impossible, silly beastie!"

The Jabberwock, now completely in Wonderland, twitched and struggled, its muscles bunching and contracting as it fought against the inevitable.

Maddie's smile dropped and her eyes narrowed. "No one hurts my dad," she said, and the tear between worlds closed.

CHAPTER 25

FRIENDS WOULD BE ♠ ACES ♣
♡ ♢

PUDDING MAKES A TERRIBLE HAT! SNOOF PIDDLE DEE-HEllo? Hello, testing, testing. Am I speaking reasonable words? No nonsense, no "crunchy lunches" and "utmost roast beef"? Yes! I am making sense again! The Narrator is back and doing a victory dance! Look out! Check my moves—I found them and I'm going to keep them. Oh yeah, *doot doot doot*—

"Narrator, you're back!" Maddie squeaked. "Yippee-potomus!"

Yes! I'm back, Maddie! That was horrible. I could

think, but my words were nonsense and I was help-less to do anything but watch the chaos and…wait, I'm the Narrator. And I'm a professional. So no more victory dancing. Back to work.

Ahem. Yes, it was a glorious day in Ever After. Even the Narrator felt glorious! The Jabberwock had returned to Wonderland, and all over the Grimmnasium, things changed by its magic were un-magicking, untangling, and unbecoming into what they used to be.

A rosebush scrunched into a tight ball like a piece of paper crumpled up in your palm. The mass of pink blooms and brown thorny branches shaped into a tall, brown-skinned, and pink-dressed girl of distin-guished height and fashion sense. She immediately ran, her high heels clacking on the Grimmnasium's hardwood floor, and barreled toward Lizzie.

"Whoa, girl, you Rockabye-Baby rock!" Briar lifted her fist.

Lizzie was still lying against the wall, but she straightened and lifted her fist. She'd watched Briar performing her signature fist bumps with her friends and so knew what to do—she knocked her knuckles against Briar's, opened her hand, and then rained wiggling fingers down in a representation of a glitter bomb. She couldn't quite suppress a pleased giggle.

"That thing was going to eat me," said Briar. "Actually going to gobble up my roses, but you wielded some seriously hextreme moves with that sword. I never knew you were so royally fablelous!"

"And I never knew that I'd bother to save your life." Lizzie cleared her throat. "I do not regret it."

"This is so wicked cool," said Briar. "Friends?"

Lizzie blinked. She looked at Briar, then at Cedar, Maddie, and Kitty.

♥

Friends are one R away from fiends.
Avoid friends at all costs!
Also anyone to whom the R does not come
naturally (pirates are okay).

♥

Sometimes her mother's advice just didn't make sense in context.

"Friends would be aces," Lizzie said.

A gold padlock lying loose clicked open, lengthened, and widened into a girl of abundant golden curls. Her wide-set curious eyes looked around, and Blondie Lockes made a noise like the snuffle of a bear.

"This is going to make the best MirrorCast show I've ever done!" she said.

A pair of crystalline shoes flashed brightly in a ray of sunlight, a swirl of sparkling light slowly resolving into Ashlynn Ella. She blinked her large doe-like eyes twice before swooning into a graceful faint. Beside her, a sturdy tree melted into Hunter Huntsman, and he caught her fainting body in one hand and his ax in the other. From somewhere unseen, trumpets played a heroic fanfare.

In midflight, a raven sprouted a head full of long purplish-black hair. She squawked and dived to the ground, alighting atop a red apple before her wings lengthened and narrowed into arms. She was fully back to being Raven when the apple sprouted back into Apple. Raven Queen was sitting on Apple White's head.

"You're sitting on my head," said Apple.

"Um…how—" Raven started before wobbling and falling off, catching herself on a bright blue bicycle just as it changed back into Dexter Charming.

No heroic trumpets played, but Dexter didn't seem to mind.

"Sorry, Dex! Thanks for breaking my fall," said Raven.

"No problem," Dexter said, his face smooshed between her boot and the floor.

Everything was reverting. Wall stones lost their wiggle, floors lost their hiss and spring. Window-panes crawled back into their frames and returned to unmoving, unblinking glass.

Even the Wonderlandians noticed slight changes, the ridiculous clarity in their brains shifting back to normal—rich and roiling with the sheer multitude of interesting things to think about, such as cabbages and kings; a large variety of hats; croquet; tea service; the best rhymes for *oranges* and *spaghetti*; and riddles like "Which came first: the chicken or the soup?" and "How much hedge would a hedgehog hog if a hedgehog could hog hedge?"

"That's such a good question, isn't it?" Maddie said. She was sitting beside the Mad Hatter, his head on her legs, smoothing his white-streaked mint-green hair off his forehead. He was awake now, and although he looked tired, he was smiling around his huge teeth.

"Indeed, my girl," said her father. "How much hedge, indeed? They do so love to hog it, and who can blame them?"

Watching it all was a real girl of warm brown skin and earnest brown eyes. She was the last to...oh, Cedar. I'm so sorry. I mean, the Narrator doesn't say *I* or feel sorry for the characters. The Narrator only observes and reports. And the Narrator observed that Cedar Wood was changing, too. *Ahem.*

Cedar felt it first in her skin. A hardening, a deadening, like water turning to ice. The change sank deeper, choking the breath in her lungs, dulling the butterfly sensation in her middle. *Thump-bump, thump-bump, thump*—The rhythm of her heart cut off midbeat, a song interrupted, and that fantastic warmness in her chest cooled. The chill exploded outward, tingling through her limbs down to the tips of her toes and fingers. Bruises disappeared, scratches mended, and at last the small cut on the tip of her index finger healed.

Though the change felt as slow as the folding up of a comforter, it all happened so fast that Cedar's wooden cheeks were still wet with tears by the time her wooden eyes could no longer cry. Her wooden nose still remembered the last real scent she'd smelled—Briar's roses.

"Cedar!" Raven clambered off Dexter and ran to give her friend a hug. "You helped save everyone! Thank you! I'm just sorry I never got to hug squishy Cedar."

"You will," said Cedar. "Someday."

"Are you going to follow your destiny, then?" Raven asked.

Cedar shook her head and heard her wooden neck creak in that old, familiar way. She sighed, a sad little huff of breath that left her wooden chest feeling empty. But she said, "Forcing things to be what they're not is so not my style. I'm more convinced than ever that everyone should be able to choose their own path. And I'm going to talk to Headmaster Grimm about it immediately. Let the Royals be Royals and the Rebels be Rebels."

"But…" Raven lifted one of Cedar's hands, running her finger across the wood grain of her knuckles.

Cedar shrugged. Her joints felt loose, so she

plucked spare pegs from her pocket and started screwing them into her elbows. "I used to think I was a piece of wood that just imagined myself a person. But now I think I'm a real person who just imagines myself made of wood."

Raven laughed. "That sounds like Wonderlandian logic."

"I've absorbed some of that, I think!" said Cedar.

She tightened the peg in her knee and tried again to hold on to the real scent of roses. She could only imagine it, and, for now, that would have to be enough. She stood straight, feeling as strong as a tree, no ache or break in her limbs. Her pain gone, her injuries healed.

Lizzie was standing and didn't show any obvious injuries from the Jabberwock's striking tail, but she looked dazed.

"Hey, Lizzie? Are you okay?" Cedar asked.

"I think I am generally sprained and significantly bruised, but, yes, I am okay." Shuffle perched on her shoulder, squeaking. "Yes, Shuffle, so long as the Grove is okay, too."

"Oh, timbersticks, that's right!" said Cedar. "Do you think the un-magicking fixed it, too?"

"I hope so, but if not"—Lizzie looked down at her shoes as if embarrassed—"at least I still have my friends."

Cedar's eyes widened, and she felt her mouth carve itself into a smile. It felt good. "If the Grove needs replanting, I'll help you, Lizzie. We all will."

Daring was fuzz-free. He bore a bruise on his cheek, but he smiled at Lizzie, his teeth brilliantly white.

Lizzie lifted one hand, posing as she had on the amphitheater's stage. "I have returned, Boreas, wind-herder, to watch you writhing in the agony of age and death."

Daring laughed heroically. "What a battle. Bards will sing of my deeds! Or perhaps a pop singer. Do you listen to Katy Fairy?"

"I do not!" Lizzie said grandly. "But I shall listen to her squalling posthaste as you are my friend, and friends recommend music to each other! Now, kneel."

Cedar was surprised to see Daring do so without argument.

Through some twist of magic, Lizzie's butter knife had enlarged with him, now as big as a sword.

She picked it up, solemnly touching its flat side to each of Daring's shoulders.

"I knight you a defender of Wonderland, Sir Daring Charming. Heroic, loyal, fuzzy doom."

Cedar creaked a smile. She looked to Raven to see if she'd observed this odd new friendship and found Raven staring up. Cedar followed her gaze to the long ripple in the air, stretching from one side of the Grimmnasium to the other. The portal to Wonderland was closed, but it had been so large it left behind a scar of piercing white light.

"Is it dangerous?" Cedar asked.

"I don't think so." Raven held her hands up, sensing the air. "It does emit a magical energy, a kind of tingle that gives me chills. I feel like it's about to—"

"Students!" Headmaster Grimm's voice shouted as the Grimmnasium door opened. He entered along with Baba Yaga and the other faculty from their field trip. "It appears our spell defeated the Jabberwock. Do not fear any longer."

Just then, the portal scar tightened, like lips pressed together. And then it exploded. The explosion was soundless, like a giant dandelion puffing out into glitter and dust. The windows blasted out, and the brilliant, glittery light burst as far away as Book End, raining sparkles and sighs over everything.

"Uh-oh, sleepy time," Briar said just before slumping to the floor.

All over the Grimmnasium everyone from Professor Rumpelstiltskin to Duchess Swan swooned into sleep. Everyone except Maddie, who looked as alert as ever.

Maddie didn't even fall asleep during the big Beauty Sleep Festival, Cedar found herself recalling as a sweet drowsiness poured over her. *Maybe it's all that tea….*Still as a tree, Cedar snoozed standing, the sprinkles of light raining over her face and arms with tiny pulses of heat and whispers of *Hush, shush, hush, shush….*

CEDAR BLINKED ONCE. SHE BLINKED TWICE. The light was gone.

Cedar could not seem to remember why she was

standing in the Grimmnasium. Or why most of her classmates were lying on the floor around her. Was this some kind of weird slumber party?

Raven was blinking, too. She pushed herself onto her elbows, staring up at the empty air.

"What are we doing?" Raven asked.

"I feel like something happened," said Cedar. "Like I was in the middle of an important thought and then...I don't know."

"Why did I take a nap on the Grimmnasium floor?" Lizzie asked.

"Welcome to my world," said Briar, yawning.

"What exactly is your world?" Lizzie asked.

"Lots and lots of unexpected naps," said Briar. "And lots and lots of unexpected parties. Ooh, we should have a party! You can come. I think. Wait...are we friends?"

"I should think not," said Lizzie. "My mother always said...friends are fiends and only pirates have *arrrrrh*s."

Briar raised one eyebrow. "Um...what?"

"What are we doing in here?" Cupid asked, flying down from the branches of a pillar tree where she'd been asleep.

"We came back early from the field trip," Cerise said, rubbing her eyes. "My dad—I mean, the faculty said there was something wrong on the mountain. Mean bears or something? I can't remember exactly."

"Right. But after that?" asked Cupid.

"I don't know," Dexter said, removing his glasses to rub the sleep from his eyes. "We fell asleep, I guess. Must've been a busy day."

Maddie was standing with her fists on her hips, staring with wide eyes. "Are you all cuckoo clocks? We had an amazing adventure! We saved Ever After and danced with chairs and wrestled monsters...and...and...painted pictures!"

"I'm sure we did, Maddie," Raven said. "Dreams are cool that way."

"But...but...my dad is here!" Maddie said, pointing at her father, who was, indeed, by her side. The Mad Hatter waved.

Cedar waved back. It seemed the polite thing to do, though she wasn't sure what would be polite to a Wonderlandian. They rarely made sense to her.

"Kitty!" said Maddie. "You must still be mindiful and memory-hoarding."

Kitty kept smiling, though her forehead scowled.

"I had lots of dreams about…about the Jab—no! Nightmares!" She shuddered, her hair fluffing. Her eyes seemed a little sorry when she looked at Maddie and said, "But they didn't really happen, Maddie. They were just dreams."

Maddie sighed, shrugged, and then twirled toward Cedar.

"Happy snappy, my dreaming Cedar Wood! What was your don't-remember-that-it-was-all-real dream?"

Cedar didn't usually remember her dreams, only the emotions that flowed from them. Whatever she dreamed during this strange nap was no exception— confusion and fear, elation and joy, and a lingering sense of hope for something that she wanted. Or didn't. What *did* she want? She rubbed the tip of her finger and whispered, "I want to be real, but I want to choose my own story even more."

And it was true, because Cedar could not tell a lie.

Cedar was sure Maddie was about to say something silly, but she didn't. She just smiled.

The headmaster was sitting up, rubbing his gray hair.

"Students, why are all the kitchen appliances

stacked in the corner of the Grimmnasium as if they had been practicing a cheerleading formation?"

After much *what happened*s and even more *I don't know*s (except from Maddie), everyone headed through the school toward the Castleteria for dinner, discovering that nothing was where it belonged. It was as if every piece of furniture and clothing, and even a few doors, had sprouted legs and run away on their own two feet.

"Which is precisely what happened," said Maddie.

The Narrator did not confirm or deny this assertion.

Maddie sighed and stomped into the Castleteria. "This is more riddle-diculous than a bald rabbit!"

"Hey, Lizzie," said Cedar. "You know, I think I dreamed about you."

Lizzie closed one eye, squinting at Cedar with the one that was painted with a smeared red heart.

"I am a princess of Wonderland. Many dream of me." She sniffed. "But I think I dreamed of you, too."

"Do you want to maybe sit together in the Castleteria?" Cedar asked.

Lizzie did not bother to respond. But as they walked down the hall, she slowed her usual brisk pace and kept in step with Cedar. Together they passed through the Castleteria doors.

"I just had the oddest thought to check the doorframe for teeth, as if it might swallow us," Cedar said.

Lizzie didn't answer. Cedar pressed her wooden lips shut, unsure if she'd said something awkward.

But then Lizzie shouted, "I am fond of hedgehogs!"

Cedar guessed that Lizzie was attempting to have a conversation. She smiled.

"I am, too," she said.

CHAPTER 26

ACCIDENTALLY BECOMING FRIENDS

THE MORNING OF THE TIARA-THALON DAWNED as pink as leprechaun tongues. Outside the Grove, the students of Ever After High gathered, dressed in running, biking, swimming, or gardening clothes. Everyone was talking, pointing, examining the horrible damage done to Lizzie's precious garden—plants wilted and gray, great claw marks slashed through the grass, trees tipped over, roots exposed. Several students gathered around the sole remaining fluxberry bush, marveling how the berries constantly shifted in color—green one moment, then twinkling into a twilight blue, magic yellow, butterfly-wing pink…

"Listen up, everybody!" said Apple White. She wore sporty white capris, a red Ever After High T-shirt, and gold-trimmed gardening gloves. "The race will begin and end at the Grove. Runners take off from here to the lake. After getting the relay scrolls from the swimmers, the bikers cross the finish line back here, where we'll all spend the afternoon working in Lizzie's wonderlandiful Grove. As the Tiara-thalon's sponsor, the Glass Slipper has generously donated gardening tools."

"The store's owners were enchanted to help when they heard about Lizzie's plight," said Ashlynn, who worked there during after-school hours. She was surrounded by a horde of hovering pixies from the Enchanted Forest who'd come to lend a tiny hand.

"How charming!" said Apple. "Lizzie will show us how to replant the uprooted trees and extract seeds, shoots, and stem cuttings from the surviving plants to regrow the ones that were lost."

Lizzie stood at the head of the crowd, holding her

scepter regally, her chin up, eyes distant. But inside, Lizzie's very large heart felt pinched. Her beautiful Grove ravaged! Some creature must have attacked Ever After High during their mysterious Grimm-nasium nap, though besides some torn clothing and misplaced furniture, the only sign of damage was in her Grove.

Cedar Wood put a hand on Lizzie's elbow and whispered, "Don't worry. I'll help you, Lizzie. We all will."

Lizzie felt certain she'd heard those words before. "Off with your head," she whispered back in the same tone someone else might say *Thank you*.

"Let's get this running, swimming, biking, planting party started, already!" said Briar. "Athletes, get in position! Hey, Lizzie, want to help me start the race with my glitter-bomb catapult?"

Lizzie's upper lip trembled with the effort to keep stiff. She very, very, very much wanted to help with the glitter-bomb catapult. But would that be unseemly? "Off—" she started.

"Oh, just help me set it up, already," said Briar.

Lizzie dropped a round, brilliantly colored glitter bomb into the launching cup.

"You do the honors," Lizzie said. "You know, in case it misfires."

"YOLOUAT!" Briar yelled. "You only live once upon a time!" She pulled the lever.

The glitter bomb flew high over the heads of the crowd and exploded into a million pieces of glitter sparkling in the morning sun.

"Ooooh," noised the crowd in unison.

The runners took off.

"It worked!" Briar hooted. "They love it!"

"They are easily impressed," Lizzie said, and then grabbed another glitter bomb. "Let's do it again."

"Woo-hoo!" Briar cranked the launch arm back. "Glitter bombardiers in the house!"

Lizzie and Briar performed a glitter-bomb fist bump. Lizzie realized what she'd just done and pulled her hand behind her back. She must be cautious if she was to avoid accidentally becoming friends with anyone—particularly Briar, who had so many friends that soon Lizzie would be in danger of sinking on a friend ship. She knew what her mother would say about that.

Briar pulled the launch lever, and another explosion of glitter cascaded over the crowd. Her laugh was loud and bubbly, and it made Lizzie want to laugh, too. Of course, her mother's card warning about friendship also made that odd allowance for pirates....

"Briar," Lizzie said, "have you considered sailing a big boat and perhaps stealing things from other boats?"

"Um...you mean, like a pirate?"

"Yes, exactly like a pirate," Lizzie said. "I would be much more comfortable speaking with you if you were a pirate."

Briar put a finger to her chin, considering, and promptly glided to the ground, fast asleep.

"Arrr, Lizzie Hearts! Have ye killed Briar Beauty?" a voice asked from behind.

Daring Charming sauntered up and saluted her. He'd been so accommodating with her pirate request that Lizzie felt certain her mother couldn't disapprove of their friendship.

"Aren't you supposed to be racing?" Lizzie asked.

"No rush," he said. "I always win. Even when I don't." He winked at her. "Ahoy, matey."

A UNICORN-DRAWN CARRIAGE LET THE SWIM-
mers off at the lakeshore. Cedar hopped out first
and jogged down to her spot on the dock. The lake
water was as blue as dwarf crystals and so still
Cedar could see the pattern of splashes a mermaid's
tail had left behind. Around her, the other swimmers were stretching. Wooden limbs never got
injured, but Cedar stretched, too, so she wouldn't
seem weird.

"I hope you do great today, Cedar," said Poppy
O'Hair, taking a place beside Cedar on the dock.
Her hair was hidden in a blue swim cap.

"You, too, Poppy," said Cedar. "You are one of
the nicest people I know."

"Wow, thanks," said Poppy. "When someone
else compliments me, I always wonder if they really
mean it, but with you, I know."

"Good day to you, Lady Wood!" Hopper Croakington II announced from her other side. He was
in his frog form for the swimming, but what if he
popped back into regular human Hopper in the
middle of the lake? As much as Cedar longed to
change into real Cedar, she didn't want it to happen
during a swimming race.

In her nervousness, she didn't realize she was thumbing the thin line on her fingertip that had shown up after their mysterious Grimmnasium nap. It looked like a scar. Like a real, human scar. But, of course, wood didn't scar. She groaned and balled her hand into a fist to hide this further proof of her weirdness.

"What's wrong?" Raven asked, padding up next to her in bare feet. She had on a purple-and-black swimming dress, a glossy black swim cap covering her hair. At the last minute, Duchess Swan had dropped out, so Raven had volunteered to fill in for that team.

"I'm tired of being weird," Cedar blurted against her will. "I just want to be normal."

"What's normal?" Raven said, tucking a rogue lock of hair back under her cap. "No one is normal."

"You—"

"I am the daughter of the Evil Queen, who rampaged and tried to destroy fairytales, and half the school thinks I'm more evil than her precisely because I'm trying not to be."

"Apple—"

"Is perfect—and isn't *that* kind of weird? She never sweats. Have you noticed that? And all the birds? It must get old having birds constantly landing all over her and pecking her adoringly. And why doesn't she ever have bird poop on her dress?"

"But...but everyone else—"

"When Hopper there gets tongue-tied, he turns into a frog," said Raven. "Briar is so determined not to miss a second of life before her one-hundred-year snooze that she stays up all night and then is napping randomly all day. Holly's and Poppy's hair grows, like, twenty feet a day. Cerise never takes off her hood. Ashlynn is all nature-girl and one with the animals and trees—unless you wave a pair of new shoes at her, and she absolutely loses her mind. Every time Hunter strikes a heroic pose, trumpets play a fanfare. Invisible trumpets. Who plays them? And why? And...and how? And I don't even have to mention Maddie. So you're made of wood and can't tell a lie. So that's a little weird. Look around! We're all weird."

Cedar did look around. She laughed. "I guess... I guess I just thought everyone else was normal-weird and I was..." She laughed again. "From inside my own head, I seem so different."

"We all do." Raven hugged her. "And we are, thank the godmother. Can you imagine how boring life would be if we weren't? Life without weirdness would have to be fake."

"Being different is what makes things real, and I'm different," Cedar said aloud without meaning to, but she didn't mind.

The crowd lining the race began cheering.

"That means the runners are close," Raven said. "We better get ready—or *you* better get ready, since Cerise is on your team. She's sure to be here any—"

"On your right!" called out Cerise to a few scattered gasps from the crowd. She was *way* ahead of everyone else.

Cedar felt the sudden instinct to take a deep breath, which was ridiculous, because she had no lungs. But she imagined herself taking a breath and somehow knew exactly what that felt like. She laughed just as Cerise planted the waterproof relay scroll in her hand.

"What's wrong?" Cerise said, huffing and puffing from her run.

"Nothing!" Cedar shouted as she splashed into the water. And it was true.

A Wonderlandiful EPILOGUE

ADELINE HATTER WAS IN THE GROVE planting Wondodendron shoots in the rich black soil. The whole school was there, even the Tiara-thalon athletes, the swimmers still wet. Maddie was about to ask Cedar to stand closer so her dripping hair would water the plant when Maddie heard an unfamiliar voice.

What voice, Narrator? Your voice is very familiar to me. And, oh, I'm tippy-toe-tapping to hear it again and it's sense-making and story-giving!

Madeline Hatter, I am the Chief Chronicler, and I—

Oh, that voice. Yes, that is unfamiliar. And so serious! I'm sorry to laugh, but serious stuff makes me feel ticklish in my ribs and hiccupy in my smile. I start to think about a serious little family of guinea pigs I once knew in Wonderland who always wore suits and ties and dresses and practical shoes and walked around, mumbling about "declining stock prices" and "society today."

Madeline Hatter, please pay attention. Things *are* very serious. Sacred rules of narration have been broken, and—

Oh no! Please don't blame my cutie-patootie Narrator! Surely you know my Narrator was doing the best possible in a skrimpippled situation. And dangerous. So dangerous! And, yes, even serious. Besides, no one remembers what happened except me!

Yes, yes, of course. Your Narrator could hardly be blamed for being garbled by the Jabberwock's magic. Now, when you stepped in—

I'm the one in trouble? Oh twinkle bats! Please don't banishment me. I know I broke lots of narration rules. Sometimes I said "I," and to get rid of the Jabberwock I narrated what wasn't exactly happening in order to make it really, really happen, which I know is a Big Bad No-No. And I got distracted and started talking about myself more than the main characters, Lizzie and Cedar. I know I'm not the main character, and I wasn't trying to be. I'm the quirky best friend; I'm the lovable sidekick; I'm the comic relief. I'm not the hero. I know this. It was all just so complicatish and worry-making, and I felt like I was wearing an extra-tight thinking cap but not just on my head. Everywhere! And—

Madeline Hatter…

…I'm sorry. I'll never step on the Narrator's invisible toes again and just stay away from the action and not make a peep and never, ever after think I could possibly be a hero.

Is she always like this?

Always.

Narrator! You've supposed to be on my side!

I am, believe me. And I will be on your side forever after. I am officially Madeline Hatter's number one fan. Now, please listen. The Chief Chronicler isn't mad at you. Or me. She's…well, I'd say, she's impressed. And grateful. And—

Stunned.

Stunned, yes, but grateful, too. This *is* serious. Seriously exciting! We have something for you.

Ahem. Madeline Hatter, you are the first non-Narrator to be awarded one of our highest honors. Although you can't see it, I just pinned to your collar the Golden Glyph, a medal honoring your bravery, quick-thinking, and impressive narrative skills.

Good golden goose eggs, really? That's tea-riffic! I wish I could give you a hug!

Chief Chronicler, if you don't mind…may I narrate The End of this story?

Yes, please, go right ahead.

And this is what happened next. *Ahem.*

PEOPLE WERE USED TO MADELINE HATTER talking to herself, so her friends hadn't thought two things about the seemingly one-sided conversation she'd been having for the past several minutes. But now something new happened. A wind batted at Maddie's hair. No one else in the Grove even felt a breeze, and yet Maddie's lavender-and-mint-green curls wisped and lifted around her head. Her skirt flapped; her hat tipped. And then she began to rise.

The draft was so powerful it completely encircled her, lifting her on a soft blanket of breezes. Floating felt like falling into the deepest down comforter, cozy and sigh-inducing.

You see, Narrators everywhere, including her own, were giving her a twenty-one chapter salute. The rustling breath of unseen books flipping through their pages created such a strong wind around her that it carried her up, up, high up in the air. The other students stood, confused and yet understanding something solemn was happening.

Cupid flew up beside her. "Are you okay, Maddie?"

"Yep, I'm good," Maddie said, spinning and tumbling in the air. "Wheeee!"

And though none of the students could remember

exactly what had happened that strange day at Ever After High, they knew *something* had. Something big. Something important. Something that Maddie had been a part of. And now they were more sure than ever that Madeline Hatter was *absotively* wonderlandiful.

Thanks, Narrator. That was fun.

Thank *you*, Madeline Hatter. And may you live Happily Ever After.

ACKNOWLEDGMENTS

Ever After is feeling like a second home now. (Hey, Narrator, I wouldn't mind summering there, if that could be arranged.) Massive thanks to Ever After High's architects and caretakers from Mattel: Cindy Ledermann, Lara Dalian, Julia Phelps, Christine Kim, Robert Rudman, Nicole Corse, Audu Paden, and Venetia Davie. Equally massive thanks to the beamish team at Little, Brown Books for Young Readers, including Erin Stein, Connie Hsu, Andrew Smith, Melanie Chang, Victoria Stapleton, Christine Ma, Christina Quintero, Tim

Hall, Mara Lander, Jenn Corcoran, and Jonathan Lopes. A round of clip-clapping for Barry Goldblatt, knight in shinny-shiny armor.

My husband, Dean Hale, is a frabjous sounding board, in-house editor, and idea-herder at the best of times, but with this book he was heavily involved to the point of absolute marvelosity. You, sir, are a sillypants of delightful degree. Extra helpings of thanks to the other sillypantslings in my life, Dinah, Maggie, Max, and Wren, whose Wonder powers the stories.

ABOUT THE AUTHOR

New York Times bestselling author SHANNON HALE knew at age ten that it was her destiny to become a writer. She has quested deep into fairy tales in such enchanting books as *Ever After High: The Storybook of Legends*, *Ever After High: The Unfairest of Them All*, *The Goose Girl*, *Book of a Thousand Days*, *Rapunzel's Revenge*, and Newbery Honor recipient *Princess Academy*. With the princely and valiant writer Dean Hale, Shannon coauthored four charming children, who are free to follow their own destinies. Just so long as they get to bed on time.

The End...
is only the
beginning!

Turn the page for an
exclusive sneak peek at
the next chapter of

A new series by
acclaimed author
Suzanne Selfors
begins with
Next Top Villain.

Swan

Song

To be born a fairytale princess is a blessing, indeed, but hers is not the lazy, carefree life that many imagine. There are numerous, important decisions that a princess must make every day.

For example, how would she like to be awoken in the morning? Should she choose an enchanted alarm clock to sing and dance around her bedroom? Perhaps her parents could employ fairies to gently sprinkle waking dust on her cheeks. Maybe she'd prefer to have a household troll ring a gong or her MirrorPhone blare the latest hit song.

Duchess Swan, a fairytale princess proud and true, chose none of those options. Instead, she liked to be awoken by her favorite sound in the whole world.

Honk! Honk!

"Don't tell me it's morning already," a voice grumbled.

Duchess opened her eyes. While the honking had come from the large nest next to her bed, the complaining had come from across the room. To her constant dismay, Duchess did not sleep alone. This was the girls' dormitory at a very special school called Ever After High, and her roommate was Lizzie Hearts, daughter of the famously angry Queen of Hearts. Lizzie was not a *morning* person. Which is why she didn't own an alarm clock.

Honk! Honk!

"For the love of Wonderland!" Lizzie exclaimed, her voice partially muffled by a pillow. "Off with the duck's head!"

Duck? Duchess frowned. *Seriously?*

"Pirouette is *not* a duck," Duchess said, sitting up in bed. "Pirouette is a trumpeter swan."

"Duck, swan, pigeon...she's *loud.*" Lizzie burrowed beneath a jumble of blankets.

"Of course she's loud," Duchess said. "She's named after a trumpet, not a flute."

Honk! Honk!

Duchess waved, to let Pirouette know that she hadn't gone unnoticed. Then Duchess pushed back the lavender silk comforter and set her bare feet on the stone floor. It was the first day of the new school chapter, and she was looking forward to her new classes. Why? Because each class was another opportunity to get a perfect grade. As a member of the Royals, Duchess took her princess duties very seriously. One of those duties was to be the best student she could be.

But there was another truth, somewhat darker and simmering below her perfect surface. Duchess Swan was well aware that grades were something she could control, while her ill-fated destiny was not.

Tendrils of warm air wafted from the furnace vent, curling around her like a hug. She pointed her toes, then flexed, stretching the muscles. It was important to keep her feet limber, for she was a ballerina, and her feet were her instruments.

Honk! Honk!

"Okay. Hold your feathers." Duchess slid into her robe, then opened the window. A gust of fresh morning air blew across her face. Pirouette flew outside, heading for the lush green meadow. A swan needs to stretch, too.

Just as Duchess tied the laces on her dress, the bedroom door flew open and two princesses barged in. "Ever heard of a little thing called *knocking?*" Duchess asked.

"Can we talk?" the first princess said. Her name was Ashlynn Ella, daughter of the famously humble Cinderella. She yawned super-wide. "It's about your alarm clock."

The second princess, whose name was Apple White, daughter of the famously beautiful Snow White, also yawned. "Yes. Your goose alarm clock."

"She's not a goose." Duchess sighed. These princesses really knew how to get under her wings. "She's a swan."

"Oh, that's right. Sorry," Apple said.

The two princesses, having just rolled out of bed, looked unbelievably perfect. No bedhead, no sheet lines, no crusty sandman sand at the corners of their eyes. Apple was known as the Fairest One of All, and Ashlynn couldn't be any lovelier, even if she tried.

"Apple and I agree, as do the other princesses, that the honking sound that comes from your room every morning is starting to become a bit of a royal pain."

Royal pain? Duchess looked away for a brief moment so they wouldn't see the twinge of hurt feelings.

"I'd be happy to lend you some of my songbirds,"

Ashlynn said. Then she whistled. Three tiny birds flew through the doorway and landed on her outstretched finger. "It's such a cheerful way to wake up."

"Bird alarms aren't always reliable," Apple said. "I'd be happy to connect you to my network of dwarves. They'll send a wake-up call to your MirrorPhone."

"I don't need your songbirds or dwarves," Duchess told them, a bit annoyed.

Okay, she was more than a *bit* annoyed. Those girls were always acting as if they were better. They really ruffled her feathers!

Ashlynn, Apple, and Lizzie were Royals—the blood daughters of fairytale kings and queens. Being a Royal at Ever After High meant being part of the most popular and the most privileged group. Duchess was also a Royal, but she was different. Most Royals were destined to marry other Royals and rule kingdoms, living out their lives in comfort, health, and fortune. In other words, a big, fat Happily Ever After was waiting for most of them.

But Duchess did not have such a future, nor did she have a future as a dancer. Her destiny, as the daughter of the Swan Queen, was to turn into a swan and live out her days web-footed and feathered.

You can't perform a graceful *grand jeté* with webbed feet!

To make matters worse, she had no Happily Ever After with a charming prince written into her story.

Although Duchess's future did not seem fair, she'd accepted her circumstances. It was her duty to keep her story alive by fulfilling her destiny. She worked hard at her studies and her dancing. She did her best to make her family proud. But it drove her crazy that these girls had nothing more to worry about than being awoken by honking. It was just as Duchess often said: Birds of a feather flock together.

Lizzie popped her head out of the covers and glared at the intruders. "I order this meeting to be over. Now!"

"Sounds good to me," Duchess said. "Even though

I was so enjoying our little chat." She forced a smile. "However, it's time to get dressed for class. And you know what happens if you're late." She looked directly at Ashlynn.

"Oh my godmother, thanks for the reminder," Ashlynn said, her eyes widening with worry. If she was even just one second late, her clothes would turn into rags. She picked up the hem of her nightgown and rushed out the door, her songbirds following.

"Well, I'd better go, too. I hear my magic mirror calling. Charm you later," Apple said.

Duchess's smile collapsed the moment the princesses were gone. "Good riddance," she muttered under her breath.

"If my mother were here, she'd order their heads chopped off," Lizzie said. Then she burrowed back under the blankets.

Just as Duchess closed the bedroom door, Pirouette flew back in through the window. She landed at Duchess's feet, then turned the corners of her beak

into a smile. Duchess knelt and gave her a hug. The wonderful scent of wind clung to Pirouette's white feathers. "Lucky girl," Duchess whispered. "You don't have to deal with know-it-all princesses."

Duchess filled a bowl with swan kibble—a mixture of breadcrumbs and grains—and set it on the floor. Pirouette began eating her breakfast. This was the calmest time of the day for Duchess, before the flurry of classes and activities, while Lizzie snored peacefully. And she usually began each day by writing in her journal.

She sat at her desk and opened the top drawer. There was no need to hide the golden book, because it was enchanted with a security spell. She pressed her fingers against the cover. A click sounded. This was the only place where she shared her truest of feelings—her darkest of secrets. After turning to a blank page, she dipped her quill into ink and began to write. But one thought filled her mind. One thought that never seemed to go away. And so she wrote:

I wish I had a Happily Ever After like Ashlynn's and Apple's.

Then Duchess Swan looked out the window and sighed. Being a perfect princess meant she had to accept her destiny, even if that destiny was covered in feathers.

Ugly Duckling

*D*uchess learned about her destiny on the morning after her eighth birthday, when she awoke and discovered that her feet had changed overnight.

It was a terrifying sight. "Grandma!" she cried. "What happened?"

Her grandmother pulled back the covers, took a peek, then sat calmly at the edge of the bed. "Dear child," she said. "This is the beginning."

"The beginning of what?" Duchess asked. She pulled her knees to her chest so she could get a closer look. Her feet, which had been normal when she'd gone to sleep, were now flat, black, and webbed. "Take them off," she said, pulling on them as if they were shoes. "Make them go away!"

"They will go away," her grandmother said. "Don't worry. You will learn how to make them come and go as you please."

But they didn't go away. They stayed while she got dressed and they stayed while she ate breakfast. She tried to squeeze them into shoes, but they wouldn't fit. "I'm not going to school like this!" Duchess insisted.

"A princess must be educated," her grandmother said, gently pushing her out the palace door. "A princess must never be ashamed of who she is."

The village kids pointed and laughed as Duchess waddled down the lane, her big, flat feet making flapping sounds. "She looks like a duck," they said. "Ugly duck, ugly duck."

She felt ugly.

The webbed feet disappeared later that day. After

school, Duchess ran home, barefoot, and didn't complain about the sharp rocks in the lane. She was so happy to have toes again!

More changes came that year. She grew taller, her legs turning as skinny and gangly as a bird's. Sometimes when she laughed, she'd honk, which made all the other kids laugh. In the mornings, she'd find white feathers in her bed.

And she began to crave the plants that grew in the pond behind the schoolhouse. Spring green and tender, they looked so delectable. One day she waded in and began to eat them. "Look! The princess has flipped her crown. She's eating weeds!" Luckily, the village children didn't notice her also eating the little water bugs that skimmed the pond's surface. They tasted just as good as the cook's roasted beast.

What is happening to me?

Then, one morning, while walking home from school, Duchess spied a downy feather floating in the wind. It looked exactly like the feathers she often found in her bed. She chased after it, then saw another, and another, drifting in the distance. The trail led her to the lake behind the palace, where a bevy of swans had gathered. Although they migrated to the palace grounds every winter, Duchess had never paid close attention to them. She knew that they were beautiful, with their snowy white feathers, black beaks, and black eyes. But as she sat in the grass, watching them preen and glide, she came to an amazing realization. Their swan feet looked exactly like the webbed feet she'd grown.

She was one of them!

And so, Duchess began to teach herself how to control the changes. It was not easy, for a sneeze could turn one arm into a wing, or a laughing fit could make a beak appear. By the time she was ten, she could control the transformation. She could turn herself into a swan whenever she wanted.

She saved this reveal for a special day at spellementary school. It was late spring and the class was lined up along the edge of the swimming pool. "Today we will learn how to do a swan dive," her teacher, Mrs. Watersprite, said, pointing to the highest board. The students lined up at the bottom of the ladder. There were many trembling legs and terrified squeals as they climbed. "This is the most graceful dive of all," Mrs. Watersprite explained. "Put your hands above your head, lean forward, and jump! Then spread your arms wide, like wings."

One by one, the students jumped. Some clawed at the air as if trying to stop the fall. Some landed on their bellies. Others went feet first. "No, no, no!" Mrs. Watersprite hollered. "That was not graceful!"

Duchess went last. She raised her arms above her head and gripped the end of the board with her toes. It was a long way down. The other students looked small, some shivering beneath their towels. With their faces turned upward, they waited for the ugly duck girl to jump.

"Dive!" Mrs. Watersprite ordered.

Duchess bounced three times, then jumped. Just as gravity grabbed hold of her, she reached out her arms, closed her eyes, and transformed.

The dive was perfection. When she rose to the surface, the village kids cheered.

And that day, the ugly duck girl became the Swan Princess.

Read more about Duchess Swan and Lizzie Hearts in the new book coming January 2015!

And don't miss the companion Destiny Do-Over Diary!